APRIL'S ABSOLUTION

APRIL'S ABSOLUTION

Final entry to April's Series

L.A. White

A.M L&C

Cover design by: Aria Blake @blakedesign
Supported by @therightbuzz
Part of Chick Lit Cafe' Marketing

As always, this goes out to friends, family, fans and my hubby...

More importantly I would like to dedicate this to my mother Sheila, my mother in law Sue and my dearest of friends Emma, Karen and Ellie. Your continued support has been incredible.

Lastly, I want to name my husband Colin. The man behind the scenes who hasn't read any of these books, but still acts like he has to take the credit for pushing me to get them all done - thanks babes! Man support one on one!

This also couldn't have been as successful as it is without the amazing guys at The Right Buzz!

CONTENTS

FOREWORD

The harder the conflict, the greater the triumph.
George Washington

PREFACE

The title April's Absolution may suggest to you that she has found forgiveness and absolution as the definition would describe. It is not: nothing about this is worth forgiveness from April. It is more in the respect that she finally finds her freedom. It is that she is finally released.

Having been through so much to get to this point, the word absolution just fit with me. It just felt right for the book and it feels right for April as well.

Her absolution is her vindication: it is her liberation.

It's all been leading up to this.

It all ends here.

CHAPTER 1

"Has she eaten anything yet?" Lucas asked Andrew, the pity on his face evident.

"No" he replied.

"Mate it's been three days: she needs to eat something soon."

"I know Ethan, but I can't force her can I?"

"Has she said much?" Jamie questioned, the look on his face mirroring Lucas's.

"Not really. She's done nothing but cry and ask why. She keeps waking up in the middle of the night in sheds of tears. I don't know what to do or to say to her anymore."

The four of them fell silent. They sat in the tech lab, it was the early hours of the morning and they had been there for most of the night. They had nothing. They didn't know where her EX was, why he was doing this and what his next steps were.

Andrew knew in his heart that everything over the last few years was leading up to this. The end game was near. Death was riding with the wind. Whose deaths he didn't know, but he felt it coming like an artic front he couldn't escape. It chilled him to the core.

"You want to head off? There's not much else we can do tonight."

Andrew looked at Lucas, well, looked through Lucas. He both wanted to go back to his room, and he didn't. At least trying to find her EX and plan his demise was something to take his mind off the situation in his room. A situation where April wasn't talking, eating or sleeping properly. It was showing as well. The cracks were opening and the woman was looking gaunter by the day.

"Hut hum."

Andrew shook his head. "Sorry Lucas, daydreaming. Yeah, I'll head back." With that, Andrew got up and left the room in silence. No worried look or feeling of unease around him would make it worse.

He walked back to his room, cursing under his breath. Why? All he wanted to know, as much as April did, was why? Why would her EX have so much hate in him? Why did he want April dead? What, if anything, had she done?

He got to his door and heard her wails of pain before he opened it. His fingers shook as they were reaching for the handle. His heart took a beating when he opened it and saw her.

She sat on the floor next to the bed with her back against the mattress and her face in her hands. Her body was wracked with sobs, shaking uncontrollably. Her black pyjamas were clinging to her body, soaked with tears.

"April, love, tell me how to help you. Tell me what I

can do?"

She didn't look up at him: she didn't stop crying. He shut his door and went over to her. He sat next to her on the floor and put his arm around her. He leant her into him and kissed her head.

"April talk to me."

She was trying to get her breath back. Trying to bring fresh air into her lungs over the spasming of her lips. Andrew had never seen anyone cry so much in his life. His heart took another beating.

"April please. You have to say something to me." He gave her a gentle shake.

She shook her head signalling that no, she didn't have to say anything, and she wouldn't.

Andrew wiped a hand down his face. He was lost in a sea of emotion, lost in the bottom of a pity well and couldn't foresee a way to get back out of it all. After everything that had happened, why was she letting him win? Each tear she shed, each meal she missed and each hour of sleep she didn't get was playing into his hands. This was what he wanted. He wanted her to hurt. He wanted her to blame herself for this and it was exactly what she was doing.

He couldn't stand it anymore. The love of his life was in agony and he couldn't fix it. Like an unreliable builder, the tools in his case just weren't good enough.

He gently let her go and got up. He walked into the bathroom and turned the water on the shower before submerging himself under the hot spray.

He shook his head. He shook his head at the situation, at the lack of his ability to comfort April: he shook his head at the world. He wanted to punch the white tiles on the wall. He wanted to do some damage to anything physical to release some of the anger in his heart.

He stood there with his head under the shower and with his eyes closed. The cold hands around his body made him jump. April had joined him and had her body pressed up against his back and her arms wrapped around his waist.

He wouldn't turn around and he wouldn't say anything. Just her touching him and her making the effort to have a shower was progress enough: he didn't want to ruin it. It would end up being one step forward and twenty steps back if he did.

"Andrew I'm so..."

"Don't say you're sorry April. I don't want to hear it." He turned in her arms and looked down at her face. She kept her eyes away from him. He put his finger under her chin to raise her face so their eyes met. Red, puffiness stared back at him. He didn't know what to say.

He moved her hands and put them around his neck. He lifted her up and wrapped her legs around his waist. He held her. He held her so tight, it was as though he was worried she would vanish if he let her go.

CHAPTER 2

"I'm worried about him." Lucas said to whoever was listening, but only after Andrew had left the room. He brushed his blonde hair back with his left hand and felt his body go slack at the severity of the situation.

"Boss I'm worried about *her* and him. Will they survive this?"

"I'm sure they will Ethan. As a couple they are strong, but all the time her EX is out there, alive and kicking so to say, they won't rest."

"I can't believe we have nothing." Ethan leant back in his chair and stretched his arms and shoulders. It had been a long night for all of them. A long and unsuccessful night.

"That's not entirely true. At least we know who it is and have a picture of him. When Blake and Richie get up in the morning I'll ask them to look through CCTV around the area. They need to check any airports, train stations, any local places he's known to have been in the past. If April wasn't so upset I'd involve her more. She must know his common go to places. She must know something we do not." Lucas replied.

"You think she did something back in the day?" Ethan's dark brows raised above his blue eyes, almost unbelieving.

"How can she not? Would you spend years trying to kill someone for no reason?"

"Well na Boss, but blondie? I hardly think she's carrying a mafia past. You sure the guy ain't just cracked he lost her?"

"Potentially, but it just doesn't feel right to me. Something doesn't add up."

"You're quiet." Ethan said to Jamie.

Jamie nodded, he *was* quiet, he was thinking.

"Not gonna answer?"

Jamie laughed, "I'm thinking. Put yourself in his shoes. What do we know? We know that the first leaders of the Hedonists were killed, Greg was a high school friend and with them the whole time, who is now also dead. They had been watching April for a while before Matt married her so he must have known Greg and the other two. He then had an affair, got another woman pregnant and April left him with nothing after the divorce. She's happy, he's not. What's the tie?"

"Someone's done his homework," Ethan laughed and Lucas smiled. Jamie really had done his homework. He was on to something.

"What's the tie? That's the key. Do we think Greg and Matt are related? Did April offend them in some way or is Matt just flat out jealous of what April and Andrew have and cannot stand by and let them win."

"I remember something. I remember Ellie telling me that after April left her EX, something happened with his new woman and she left him too. He then lost his job and was living in squalor."

Lucas leant forward, "when did she tell you this?"

"Months ago now. I reckon that's the reason for it all now, but why marry her in the beginning. April was a target before her EX had an affair. From the wall," Ethan gestured to the tech lab wall that had a running commentary of texts and pictures from a timeline that span over the best part of fifteen years, "this guy was always going to marry April but he mentioned it would only be for a few years before, and to use his words 'offs fatty'. Why didn't they do it after two years, why stay with April for thirteen years?"

Lucas knew Ethan was right. The reasoning for wanting April dead now, was not the same as why they wanted it back then. Why? Why go to all that trouble to pick her out, marry her, stay with her longer than intended, cheat on her and then try to kill her even more than an auction as they had planned?

"Well, now I've given everyone food for thought, I'm off to bed mate. I'm going to dip my wick in my woman." Ethan stood, stretched out his shoulders again and yawned. He walked out leaving only Jamie and Lucas shaking their heads. He would have had a fat lip if Ellie heard him say that.

"What now Lucas?"

"I don't know Jamie. I just don't know anymore.

This is twisted beyond anything I would ever imagine."

"It's a bit fucked up mate I won't deny that, but whether they wanted her dead in the beginning for some unknown reason, and why they want her dead now is semantics isn't it?"

"What do you mean semantics?"

"It's by the by. They want her dead; we need to kill them first. Reason or no reason that's what needs to happen right?"

Lucas nodded, Jamie was right. For whatever reason, it didn't really matter. They knew who was behind everything and what their end goal was. How they got there didn't really matter anymore. They need to be stopped and that was it, everything else was just a waste of time thinking about.

Lucas stood, "I'm also off to bed but I doubt I'll be getting any action tonight." He winked at Jamie; Jamie laughed in return.

"You're lucky you have a woman mate, it's been me, Mrs Palm and her five daughters for the last four years."

Lucas burst out laughing, "I bet she's reliable though?"

Jamie waved a Jazz hand at Lucas, "that she is."

As Lucas left the room, Jamie got up and looked at the wall. What were they missing? There was something else. Something else that linked everything together. Something else that was behind this all.

Matt picked out April and when Malcolm found

out it was her, he questioned why. His abrupt answer was a mere 'easy to control'. What was the purpose of having someone easy to control if you were just going to kill them anyway? Jamie knew there had been a few auctions dotted around after Amelia's and that it didn't really kick off or leave an imprint on Prevention until Silvia, so why April?

He stood there for a while longer, just looking up and down the pictures, reading through the message print outs Richie and Blake had put next to the red string, and shook his head. He'd been around long enough to know that sometimes, questions don't really have the answers you want or are looking for. Jamie wouldn't be surprised if April was just in the wrong place at the wrong time and then her fate was sealed.

Jamie yawned and looked at his watch. It was four in the morning. He needed some rest before the day he had ahead of him. He was still in training with the new recruits and each day was taking its toll. Up at nine for circuit and suicide runs around the gym: evenings reading through policies and procedures and then nights of being in the tech lab trying to solve the mystery that even Sherlock would have had headaches over. What a week: what an absolute week of shit. He left and pretty much yawned all the way to his room until his head hit the pillow.

CHAPTER 3

Ellie rolled over and accidently jabbed her elbow in Ethan's eye. He shot up and started squealing in pain.

"What the hell was that for?" he said as he rubbed his eye socket.

"Sorry babe I didn't mean to. I stretched and you were too close to me."

"Hmm, yeah sure, that or it's silent payback for the blow job comment when I got back last night."

Ellie laughed, "even though your vulgar words woke me up, I wouldn't blind you for asking for a bit of how's your father."

He winked with his good eye. He nodded his head towards his crotch and smiled.

"Are you serious?"

"Why not," he said as she got out of the bed.

"I have a job interview remember. I'm going to be late at this rate."

"Oh yeah, I totally forgot about the chef position. Go get em tiger."

"Thanks. Is it wrong I'm nervous?"

"Ells babe, you're going for an interview for a job you know you can do, and pretty much have it in the bag. Why are you nervous?"

"I haven't had an interview for a long time, and I still have my broken hand don't forget." She showed him her bandaged fingers. "I'm not exactly at best capacity right now, am I?"

"You're talking bull babe. Bad hand or not, you got the job if you want it and I'm sure the girls will help out until you're back to full whack."

She smiled, "you know, you can be really sweet sometimes, in your own weird and wonderful way."

"Weird and wonderful are my middle names girl, now get your clothes off and come and service me. The man needs attention."

Her eyebrows lowered and she scowled at him. She turned on a huff and went into the bathroom.

"Guess I'll sort myself out then shall I?" he shouted and a slam of the bathroom door was her reply. He laughed. It was such an easy thing to annoy her, and nothing more made his day. She'd be furious most of the morning with him but the makeup sex would *so* be worth it.

He leant back after giving his eye one more rub with the heel of his hand and yawned. He was knackered. All these nights on just four hours sleep were affecting his ability to think straight. What did he have on today?

His phone started buzzing on the bedside table next to him. He leant over and grabbed it before it fell on the floor.

"Hello?"

"Ethan."

"What's up small dick?" he smiled; he could practically hear Andrew's eye roll.

"Planes, clouds, Superman!"

"Did… did you just crack a joke?"

"It has been known Ethan, though I don't make a habit out of it."

Ethan laughed, "and what's brought this on. I thought you were swimming in turmoil over blondie. Hold on, she's making progress isn't she?"

Ethan heard Andrew leave a room and a door shut behind him. "She is. She showered with me yesterday and we had a long talk last night. I think she realises he is winning all the time she lets him affect her the way he has been. We're heading down to breakfast soon."

"Good news if there ever was any muckka. Ells is just getting ready for her interview with Lucas for Chris' role so I'll meet you there once I've showered."

"Shit, I forgot she was interviewing for that today. Wish her luck, though I don't think she'll need it."

"Will do, ear and small dick…" Ethan waited for Andrews heavy breathing to slow down.

"Yes," he replied through gritted teeth.

"Tell apes it's good to have her back."

"Will do." He hung up.

Just as Ethan stopped talking, Ellie came out of the bathroom in a black skirt suit with her face full of natural looking makeup and her pixie cut was gelled in an upwards quiff.

"Twit fucking twoo."

She gave a twirl, "you like?"

"Absolutely. You look stunning. A little over dressed for the role but I like it."

"I won't wear this in the kitchen you bonehead but I am a firm believer of making a good impression on an interview, and that starts with the dress code."

Ellie walked over to the wardrobe and took out some slinky black heels. Ethan got out of the bed and walked over to her. He took her in a bear hug and she wriggled to get free.

"Get off me," she muffled into his big chest.

He let her go and kissed her forehead. "Go show that Boss who's Boss."

She laughed and left.

As she was walking to the interview room on the ground floor near the big, revolving, glass double doors, she started biting her bottom lip. Why *was* she nervous? She knew Lucas and Richie who would be doing her interview. She also knew she pretty much had the role if she really wanted it, but it all felt so formal.

A few of Preventions Soldiers gave a wolf whistle as she walked down the stairs, and another looked as though he had never seen a woman in a suit before. His colleague nudged his shoulder, "wipe the dribble mate that's Ethan's bird." The guy straightened his shoulders and looked away, his cheeks going crimson as he did. Ellie laughed but liked the ego boost.

She reached the interview room and knocked.

"Come in," it was Lucas' voice.

Ellie took a huge lung full of air and blew it out slowly. She opened the door and was surprised to see how informal it was. It was just a white walled room with a filing cabinet in the corner and a round table with six chairs. Lucas sat in his usual black uniform and shaggy blonde hair and Richie looked as though he had just got out of bed, with tired dark rings around his eyes and a navy hoodie that swamped his torso. They sat two seats away from each other leaving only one seat Ellie could sit on.

"Sit: and why do you look so nervous." Lucas smiled.

"I don't know. Maybe it's because I haven't had a job interview for a while."

"Well, we're all friends here, it's really going through the processes if I'm honest. I won't do introductions; you know who we are and what we do. I have Richie with me today as he has your paperwork ready. Should you be successful that is." Lucas winked at Ellie. Finally her nerves were easing.

"So, may I ask what made you apply for this position?"

Ellie looked at her hands, now sat on top of the round table in front of her. "Well, I feel I would be a good match with the staff as I pretty much know them already, but I have had catering experience before."

"You have? I thought you worked as a florist?" Lucas seemed surprised to hear this, like she was better suited for the role than he had initially thought.

"I do now but before that I worked in a hotel for a long time as a supervisor. It called for a lot. Stepping in for front of house when they needed it, covering sickness in both the cleaning department and the kitchen. I helped cater for the weddings there as well."

Lucas smiled and gestured for her to go on.

"I also do all of my own cooking back home, well, I did until I decided to stay here more often with Ethan."

"What did you used to cook for yourself."

Ellie raised a brow, she hadn't been expecting Richie to ask her anything, the question also took Lucas back a bit.

"Anything and everything. From Mexican to roast dinners, to homemade soups and stew."

Richie smiled. "I'm sold," he said to Lucas who also smiled.

"Ellie let's get down to business. You know how tough things are at the moment. Not only was Chris killed but the entire kitchen team was taken out with him. If you take this job, *you'll* be the kitchen lead. That means the ordering, the meal planning, the leading of the team and the cleaners will also come under your department."

She nodded.

"I know you can handle it, well, when your hand

is better that is, my main concern is I don't have a team to give you right now."

"Can I suggest something?"

Lucas nodded for her to go on.

"Would you be bothered if I tried to create my own team?"

"In what respect?"

"I have a couple of friends that have been dying to leave their workplace and I know you guys pay well here. They'll be great for it."

Lucas sat in thought. He wasn't sure about this. Prevention has a vital role in the country, are highly involved with a lot of private data and there is a target on anyone's back that joins. But Ellie, the same as Vicky and April were outsiders and settled in well. And let's face it, what the hell did he have to lose? He didn't have any other option.

"Ok, let's say I say yes to you bringing in your own team. Who are they?"

Ellie smiled and perked up a little. She'd been speaking to her friend Cady lately who had been dying to know more about Ethan and leave her current employer.

"I have one person in mind at the moment. My friend Cady. She's got experience the same as me and she isn't stupid. I know you're worried about taking someone on who might spill what we do here, and who could be another target for the Hedonists, but you won't have to worry about her."

"Ok, so the job is yours if you want it and we'll bring your friend in for an interview. How's that sound?"

"I'm in." She stretched her good hand out and shook Lucas's over the table.

"Welcome, officially, to the team. Richie can you finish off here please? Ellie I'll see you later."

Lucas left and Ellie smiled from ear to ear as he walked out of the door and away to wherever he was needed.

"That was painless." Richie smiled, "but this might not be..." he walked over to the filing cabinet and took out a huge paper folder. He plonked it on the desk and Ellie's left brow rose.

"Contracts, policies and procedures, waivers." He stated.

Ellie's right brow rose to match the left.

She sat in awe at how much paperwork there was as Richie pulled out one manual after the other.

He slid a contract and a pen over the table to her.

"Page one to eight has formalities. Title, pay, annual leave entitlement and overtime procedures. There's also a job description and I've added a page with all the passwords and details for the wholesalers. You have a list of the cleaners and their contact details as they will now be responsible to report to you. Have a quick look through and if you're happy, sign the bottom of page nine."

Ellie looked at the front page. In clear, bold, black ink was her new position. Facilities manager. Next to that was the pay. She smiled, never in her life did she imagine being on a thirty grand a year salary with thirty days holiday. She made quick work of looking through her job description as she had a good idea of what she was about to sign herself up for and inked her signature on the dotted line on page nine.

She slid it, and the pen, back to Richie who smiled and popped it back in the folder. He then handed her three large manuals.

"Read through these in your own time, though I am sure you know our confidentiality policy and what to do if shit goes tits up?"

"Yep, unfortunately I *definitely* know what to do if shit hits the fan."

"Lastly, I would usually give you a key to your own suite, but I assume you'll be staying with Ethan?"

She nodded. He did too, as though he expected what her answer was already going to be. "So, here's the rest of your passes. This key card allows you access to all rooms if we're on lockdown, it doesn't happen a lot, but this is the only thing that will get you in and out if it does. You have this bunch as well..." he took out a large ring full of keys from the bottom draw in the cabinet. "I'll let you figure out what goes to what, but they are all for the kitchen. Some for your food stores, some for the walk-in freezer if it ever needs to be locked and the rest are for some of Chris's cabinets in the back room. He used to keep rigid files on his staff, doing appraisals and the like. He really did run it like a ship."

They both took a second to remember Chris and how well he did everything: remembering how much passion he put into every ounce of his role.

"That's us done then." Richie smiled and put his hand out for her to shake. She shook it and felt a weight leave her body. Why *had* she been so nervous? Ethan was right, she pretty much had the job already, what they needed to do today was to follow procedures, nothing else.

Ellie stood with her paperwork in her arms. "I'll see you later then I guess, oh actually, when does this start?"

Richie laughed, "Lucas has asked Nigel and the guys to carry on for a while until your hand gets better but I suggest you see if they need some guidance."

Ellie laughed, "got you. Thanks again." She turned and left, headed for the kitchen: her new workplace: where she was expecting to meet Ethan.

CHAPTER 4

"Andrew I'm worried about going down to the kitchen." Andrew turned back to April before he left their room. He wanted to walk over to her and brush the stray stands of her blonde hair away from her face but dared not. Her piercing blue eyes glistened as though they would release tears at any moment.

"Why love?"

"Everyone must think I'm a baby. Look how much I've let that shit-stain ruin my week."

Andrew laughed, "nice label by the way, and trust me, you've only done what everyone else here would do, and that's taken time to process. They've all been asking about you. They've missed seeing you around."

"And Ellie and Vicky? I haven't even answered their calls."

"Love, they are your sisters, surely they will understand."

She looked to her feet. She nodded. Of course they would understand. They were family.

"Then what are we waiting for?" she pushed past Andrew and walked out of the room. He followed her after locking their door and didn't say a word until they hit the kitchen.

Andrew's chin dropped to the floor and April laughed so hard, everyone in the kitchen stopped to see where the noise was coming from.

"Whooooo, she's back guys." Ethan shouted out. Vicky came running over to her and wrapped her sister in the strongest hug she could give. She kissed her cheek, "it's good to see you Ape's."

April and Vicky let each other go and April smiled, "you to sis. Now what the bloody hell happened?"

Vicky rolled her eyes, "don't ask, though you can probably guess from the state of our other sister."

That was true, from the looks of it, Nigel had been carrying a two stone bag of flour through to the back room and dropped it at Ellie's feet by mistake. The floor was covered in flour which resembled a fresh dusting of pure white snow. Ellie's black outfit was covered in patches of white as though she had been standing in that snow for the best part of an hour and somehow, it was even in her hair. Nigel stood with a wet cloth trying to get the worst of it off her while Ethan was doubling up in hysterics, as the more water Nigel put on Ellie's clothes, the more the flour was turning into a glue-like substance and was going nowhere. Damage control gone very, very wrong.

The entire kitchen was in uproar and Nigel looked as though he wanted to die, right there on the spot. If his cheeks burned any hotter with embarrass-ment, he'd set the smoke alarms off.

Ellie looked over to April, smiled and shrugged her shoulders as if to say, 'never a dull moment in this mad house,' and then proceeded to stop Nigel from making matters worse.

Lucas and Amelia arrived with Drew in toe and before Lucas could say anything, Ellie let out a massive whistle.

"Right everyone listen," she hollered at the top of her range. "I need volunteers to clean this up, Nigel, love you to bits but get that bloody cloth away from me and go and clean up, then come back and check on the eggs and bacon, you..." she pointed to one of the other Prevention Soldiers that was stirring some beans, "get the plates ready at the end and tell your buddy next to you to start getting everything in serving dishes."

Lucas lowly whistled and put his hand on Andrew's shoulder, who had stood gobsmacked at the entrance to the kitchen, taking in the scene in front of him.

"She got the job and by that reaction, she's going to take it by storm." Lucas said so April and Andrew could hear.

April turned around and smiled at Lucas and then gave Amelia and Drew a quick kiss on the cheek.

"It's good to see you hun," Amelia said.

"You too, it's nice to finally be out of that room you know."

"I know what you mean: say no more. Let's find somewhere to sit for a bit. Lucas do you mind?" Amelia went to hand Drew over.

"Hold that thought love, I need to speak with Ellie quickly."

Amelia frowned but carried on with Drew in her arms.

Lucas ran over to Ellie, "I wasn't expecting you to have to pitch in till your hand is better but thank the heaven's you took the role."

"It's not a worry and trust me, when that delivery turned up and I saw Nigel looking like a lost sheep I had to say something, and then now look at me." She gestured to the state of her suit.

"A sign of times to come I feel."

"You got that right, though if I learned anything from Chris, it's that I won't be taking no shit and this place will run as smoothly as if he were here."

Lucas smiled. "That's a lovely thought. Good luck, and er, maybe you should change before you eat?"

Ellie burst out laughing, "I'll get through this first and then I'll change, who knows what'll be spilt over me by the time breakfast is over."

Lucas gave her an army salute before joining Amelia, Drew, April and Andrew at one of the larger tables. All of them avoiding the flour scene as each of them were in black. He sat and smiled. April seemed her usual self: she was laughing with Amelia and playing with Drew and looked in her element again. Hopefully it stayed this time.

He leant over to speak quietly to Andrew, "she seems better?"

"She does, though I'm not going to get my hopes up too much. She doesn't know our lacking efforts in finding her EX, but she does realise she can't let him ruin her life more than he has."

"I might pull Jamie out of training today. I want him to do some searches with Richie and Blake."

"You think he'll have better joy?"

"Yes and no. Blake and Richie are great at what they do, Jamie just has that eye for detail. He might be able to filter through the data and see something we haven't. After all, it was him that told Richie and Blake not to ignore her EX from the files *we* archived." Lucas shook his head.

Andrew knew that look. Lucas's face said it all. "Don't start blaming yourself for this."

"What if we had taken some more time to look into him and not dismiss him. We might have found him sooner and stopped some of our guys getting killed."

"How Lucas? We only really suspected him after the wedding, nothing we could have done would have stopped the way it all played out."

Lucas huffed, "I just wish I could do more. We still haven't had the time to have Chris's funeral yet. I hate the thought of him and his team lying waiting in our morgue."

Andrew turned in his chair and faced Lucas head on. "I think it's better that April can attend the funeral. In a way, I'm glad you didn't have it when we were in Italy: I think, well, I hope, it'll give her some closure. Also, you've done more than enough. Don't start dwelling on what could have been. All the 'what ifs' will lead to a path you don't want to get lost on." Andrew raised his brows. It was a silent command telling Lucas to get his head out of his arse because nothing anyone could have done would have stopped anything: including the infamous leader of Prevention, no matter how trained and ruthless he was!

Lucas nodded, then rolled his eyes as Ethan started walking over, still belly laughing at the state of his misses.

"Oh my days that was hilarious. Have you ever seen so much white before? I didn't know whether to bake a cake or start riding the white pony," he carried on laughing.

Right at that moment, Ellie came over and slapped him round the back of the head.

"Ow, what was that for?"

"You're a putz you know that, a big, ignorant putz." She put her good hand on her hip, scowled at him and then walked off to help finish off the last of the work before their breakfast could be served.

Ethan rubbed the back of his head and looked sheepishly to Lucas and Andrew, who were now trying not to laugh as hard as Ethan had been. Even April was stifling a laugh behind the hand covering her mouth and Amelia's eyes were rolling at everyone.

Ethan sat down next to April and he pulled her into his side. "Missed ya blondie."

She smiled as he let her go, "missed you to. I missed everyone. Even though it's only been three days it feels a lot longer than that."

"Mate, three days without the pleasure of seeing me is a death sentence. How have you coped with just a small dick for company?"

Andrew growled: Ethan laughed.

"I've managed without you Ethan. Sorry to say, but you're not the God in my history." April gave a wink to Andrew.

Ethan rolled his eyes. "Blah blah blah. Borrrrrring."

"Ethan," Lucas gave his one, stern word and Ethan knew to shut the hell up. If Ellie doesn't black his eye by the end of the day, Lucas will.

"Got ya. So anyway, where's Mr Keen?"

"I assume you're asking about Jamie," Lucas questioned.

"I am."

"I don't know actually. Mind you, I left the tech lab this morning before he did. I don't know how much longer he stayed after I left."

"Grubs up everyone," Ellie shouted from the side lines of the kitchen. She now had a white pinafore over her dusty suit.

Ethan rubbed his hands together and was just about to get up when Lucas said, "hold your horses Ethan. Let the new recruits and everyone else get their food first. I need words with you all after they have gone."

"Ain't *I* meant to be training the new recruits today?"

"You were, but I am planning on them having a day to rest." With that, Lucas stood up to address the room.

"Prevention recruits, you will not be having any training today. Eat your breakfast and then take the day for yourselves."

There was a symphony of cheers and whistles as he sat back down. A day off is what they needed, not just the recruits either, everyone needed time to rest but Lucas couldn't grant the leader team the same benefits. *They* had work to do.

Jamie arrived at the kitchen with Steve next to him. They had been becoming quite close lately as they both had a fondness for an early morning run. By the looks of their red faces, they had not long finished.

Steve left Jamie's side to go and see Vicky as she was helping dish out some food for the Soldier's waiting, not so patiently, in line for their grub. Jamie walked towards the group and took a seat.

"Morning everyone, April, lovely to see you again."

April nodded and smiled.

"Morning dude," Ethan replied and everyone else smiled at Jamie.

Jamie was a part of the group, a part of them all now, and any formalities had long gone since he proved his worth. A vital player in the midst.

"Dare I ask about the cocaine looking substance on the floor?"

"I wouldn't. Long story short, Nigel can't carry flour into a room without throwing it everywhere." Ethan laughed.

Jamie looked as though that was answer enough: he wouldn't press the matter further.

Steve came over to the table holding Vicky's hand and the both of them sat down on the spare seats. "April," he nodded and smiled to her.

April smiled back to Steve and winked at Vicky.

April was ever approving of her sister's choice in a companion. Steve was a good guy, a reserved guy and a perfect match for Vick. Mind you, though Ethan was an idiot sometimes, he too was the perfect match for Ellie.

Then there was Andrew. No one suited April better, no one could have seen her through such a tough time the way he had. He's protected her, he's bent the knee for her so many times and all she does is keep putting him and everyone she loves in harm's way. That was why she had been in her room crying, that was why she couldn't get over what her EX had been doing. She was the reason so many people were dead: she was the reason Chris was no longer here.

Out of nowhere April's eyes started to fill with tears. She couldn't get over the guilt she was feeling. She couldn't push it aside and live a normal life. She needed revenge: she needed absolution.

Andrew coughed in her direction, seeing the look on her face and knowing what was coming.

"Let's get our food shall we, love?"

April nodded to Andrew: scared that if she speaks her voice will crack and everyone else will know she is at breaking point. Andrew stood and held his hand out and April gladly put hers in it when she stood and reached him. His presence, the mere warmth of his hand gave her comfort.

They walked towards Ellie and the serving hatches, and he whispered in her ear, "are you ok?"

"I'm trying to be."

"I know, I can see this is hard for you. Stop worrying about everything that has happened. You can't change it; it wasn't your fault and you need to stop feeling so guilty."

She looked up at him. No words would ever be enough to tell him how much he means to her. No actions would show it. Knowing now was not the right time, she tiptoed to reach his face and gave him a gentle kiss on his chin. She wanted, no, yearned, to do so much more.

He put his arm around her waist and gave her a little squeeze. He didn't need to hear any words from her either. They knew how much they loved each other; they knew nothing would ever tear them apart. As though fate had etched their destinies in the old books, their lives were as one.

The line for the food started to filter down and it was their turn to grab their plates. By this time the rest of the crew had joined them, only Lucas stayed behind keeping an eye on Drew. Amelia would get his plate for him.

Upon everyone getting their food and Ellie satisfied that each had what they needed, did she grab a plate for herself and join the group at the table.

"This looks incredible Ellie," Jamie said before he started eating his full English breakfast.

"Thank you, though I won't take all the credit, poor

Nigel did most of it."

"You just arrived in time to get a flour shower," Ethan laughed.

"Give over will you. I don't know if I have the energy for you today." Amelia glared at him. She got a tongue full of food from him at that comment.

Like a mimic, Drew started sticking his tongue out with a mouth full of food as well and everyone laughed: bar Lucas that is.

"No bubba, we don't eat our food like that. Only children do that and you're far more superior to the talent we have around here." Lucas aimed at Drew, but they all knew who that comment was really for. Amelia laughed as Ethan's cheeks went bright red.

All went quiet for a while as everyone was tucking into their own plate full of food. April practically wolfed hers down without it touching the sides. Andrew looked at her in approval. It was about time she had something to eat. No wonder she was ravenous. It'd been nearly four days.

"Feel better? I don't think I've ever seen you eat so fast, and I saw how hungry you were after your training with Ethan?" Amelia giggled at April.

April smiled back, "not going to lie, I could literally eat that again."

"Why don't you get seconds, there's plenty to spare." Ellie suggested.

"I'll see what happens with everyone else first, I don't want to be the woman in the camp who's known to eat more than the blokes."

"I highly doubt anyone will care," Vicky encouraged, knowing her sister looked like she needed seconds, maybe even thirds.

"In time. So what's everyone been up to since I was incognito?" April said to change the topic of her eating habits.

"Not too much, training, planning, working and thinking. The usual," Jamie commented.

Everyone else nodded in agreement.

"Speaking of working and planning, I need you all to meet me in the tech lab after we finish here."

"Men, women, or both Boss?"

"Just the men for now Ethan, I am sure the ladies would like some time to catch up. Amelia where is Sheila?"

"She's at the back of the room eating with the rest of the cleaning staff, why?"

"It might be nice to ask her to look after Drew while you and the girls have some time together. I am sure there is still a stash of alcohol left from the wedding." He winked at her: her face lit up like she'd just been given free rein to cause carnage.

"I like your thinking. What say you girls? Bit of catching up with some cocktails?"

"I'm in," April smiled, Vicky nodded, not wanting to speak with a mouth full of food and Ellie did the same.

"I need to change though girls," Ellie said after she had swallowed her forkful.

"You don't want to get floury glue all over the seats in the common room?"

"Now you say it Amelia, sounds like a great idea?" Everyone laughed before each male started picking up their partners empty plates and putting them on the side for the porter crew to take care of. Andrew walked back over to the table as Ethan and Lucas had a private moment with Jamie and Steve at the kitchen food hatch, and kissed April on the head. She briefly leant into his lips and felt as though any separation from him would be too much, but even *she* couldn't deny she needed some girl time.

"I'll see you tonight love."

She nodded and smiled as he walked off.

Lucas had finished saying what he needed to, to the other men and came and took Drew from his highchair.

"Till later love, I'll go and arrange for Sheila to have bubba here."

"Cheers dude!"

Lucas raised a brow to his wife. It silently said two words... Dude? Really? She simply shrugged her shoulders in return.

As the rest of the Soldier's finished up their meals, and with the guys giving some half-arsed waves at their females, and with Drew now safely in Shelia's capable hands, Ellie stood to leave.

"Girls, take this key. The dark one will open the booze cupboard. Everything you need to get us sorted is out the back as well. I'll be back once I've sorted Nigel and the team out and got dressed in something that doesn't resemble a Police drugs locker."

Amelia, April and Vicky laughed.

"Congratulations on the role by the way, you'll be amazing."

"Thanks Apes, now I just have to tell my old employer I'm offskies and that's that." She said as she walked off to find Nigel and the clean-up team.

"I don't want to ask you too much until Ells get back, but are you ok Apes?"

"I'm ok Vicks, just bewildered you know." She admitted. She was still finding it hard to learn that after all the time she spent with her EX-husband, she had no idea what he had planned for her. Who he really was?

"I get it. I can't believe it if I'm honest. Steve told me who it was. Matt," she tutted, "what a bastard."

April smiled: she felt the same. What an absolute bastard indeed.

"Enough of this ladies, I feel a party coming on." Amelia grabbed the keys off the table where Ellie had left them, she gave Ellie a wide berth as she didn't want to get covered in flour and moved around Nigel and the blokes that were cleaning the kitchen up.

Ellie left and Amelia waited at the main cooking station, looking at April and Vicky as if to say, 'well hurry up then.'

Vicky and April finally got up and joined Amelia. They went into the back room where Chris had his old office and noticed the dark wooden booze cupboard. It resembled an old bureau for paperwork.

They opened it up with one of the smaller keys and Amelia let out a "whoop whoop: jackpot."

Inside it, bottle after bottle of strong alcohol was lined up by colour of liquid. Clear gins, rums and vodkas were on the top shelf, darker rums, brandy's and whiskeys lined the second shelf and the bottom shelf had all of the shotting alcohol and the coloured liquors. They were in for a treat: a very strong and boozy treat.

"Ape's grab the biggest bowl you can find, Vicks you're on ice and mixer duty, I've got this little baby under control," Amelia said as she started taking bottle after bottle off the shelves. She poured more than the recommended amount of gin, vodka, malibu and blue curacao into the bowl that April had managed to find, then poured in just a small amount of lemonade and filled it with ice.

She gave it a stir, took a ladle to it and tasted it. "Whoa, that'll put hairs on your arse mate I'm telling you."

April and Vicky were cracking up at Amelia's face. Picture someone eating the sourest fruit while standing on a piece of Lego and you had Amelia's expression down to a tee. Her grey eyes were wide and her cheeks were reddening already.

"I don't know what you're laughing at, this is just cocktail number one. More will follow," she winked at them.

As they put the kitchen back to normal, Ellie walked in, in fresh new jeans and a rock band T shirt.

"That looks nuclear. Let's get cracking." She guided Amelia out of the back room, grabbed some glasses off the shelf and led the way to the common room. "This ladies, is about to get savage." Ellie said, and all four of them laughed in agreement. Certainly savage.

CHAPTER 5

It had only been a few days, but a few days couch surfing on Jo's double suite like a homeless prick was infuriating him. How had his life gotten so bad? He was living the dream fourteen years ago. Though April was a target, he didn't expect to fall in love with her the way he did, and the group was certainly pissed off with him that he stayed with her so long. If she hadn't had heard his conversation with his mistress, he would probably still be with her now. Especially as Mike, Marcus and Greg were dead. They were no longer around, telling him he was a waste of space and couldn't follow through with his plans. On the flip side of that, their demise left him in charge of the Hedonists and he'd turned them into a revenge seeking organisation, instead of the highly skilled killing team they were meant to be. They were dropping like flies.

He sat up on Jo's couch, pushed the tattered blanket off him and rubbed his eyes. He wasn't sleeping well. Asides from Jo's one bed apartment being cold, all the time, and with everything being so white in the building the sunlight caught it first thing in the morning and blinded his eyes till they watered, but he had been constantly thinking about her. April: who wasn't intended to be the love of his life, but is: who also wasn't intended to be his wife for so long, but it happened: who wasn't supposed to still be alive, but was.

Why did she have to fall in love with that bloke. If Andrew hadn't of met April and filled her mind with bullshit and promises of a better life, he would have had the chance to get back with her. He wouldn't have lost his home, his job, his mistress and eventually, when the time was right, he could have kept to his word and auctioned her off the same as the rest, the way the plan was meant to have been played out. But, it didn't go that way did it. She heard the call, she met that prick, she left him with nothing and now his life isn't worth the measly twenty quid he has in his pocket.

What was he going to do now? There was still only one thing he wanted from all of this and that was to kill April and her new squeeze. How though? Every plan in the past had gone terribly wrong. He'd underestimated her new crew and their capabilities. They'd managed to get themselves out of the situation time and time again, and all he got from it all was death on his hands. Not that he cared. He didn't give any of the Hedonists a second thought after they died. He didn't even go to any funeral. Why should he. He was in charge, he set the tone. If they had all followed orders, down to the very word like he'd wanted them to, they would have come out on top a lot sooner.

He heard Jo's alarm go off in the other room. He rolled his eyes. As handy as Jo was, he was a buffoon. A classic meat head that worried more about how many steroids he could take to increase the mass of his arm muscle, than use a single brain cell to be useful.

Jo surfaced and walked into his lounge in his underwear.

"Didn't fancy putting on any clothes? Do you think I like seeing you walking around like that?" Matt tutted at Jo.

"Forgot you were here actually." Jo replied, but what he really wanted to say is 'it's my house and I will wear whatever the hell I want.' He didn't though. He wouldn't. He wouldn't dare.

Jo walked over to his desk where his laptop was and took the black dressing gown off the back of his wooden chair. He wrapped himself up and sat down on the remaining single seat.

"How long have you been awake?" Jo asked him.

"Not long, though it's hard to get any sleep around here at all with your white walls and lack of heating."

"I can put the heating on, I just don't want to spend more money on the bill each month."

"Forget it: I will not be here longer than I need to and definitely not longer than a month."

"You have a plan yet then?"

Matt sat in thought. Did he? Did he have a plan?

He slowly nodded to Jo and smiled such a wicked

smile Jo swallowed in fear.

"I'm going to lure her out. I'm going to get them in a location *I* choose, and then I'm going to kill her bloke in front of her and shoot her in the head. Simple, but effective."

"How are you going to do that?"

"You. You're going to get a message to her, once she has it she'll do what I ask and then it's just a game of bye bye."

Jo sat in thought. How would he get a message to her? That building was breached more than once by the Hedonists on Matts orders, Jo doubted he would get anywhere near her now.

"How?"

"Leave that to me. I'll think of something."

"And what message am I supposed to tell her?"

He looked at Jo. If the look wasn't frightening enough, his words were.... "That I will kill every single person outside of that compound unless she meets me."

CHAPTER 6

All men entered the tech lab together, to find Richie and Blake having a hushed discussion in front of one of the white boards. They were so into what they were doing they hadn't even noticed they had company until Lucas coughed.

Blake turned around, "sorry Boss: didn't see you there."

"I know," Lucas smiled. "So, what has your attention so focused?"

Richie finished writing something on the white board, turned and gave a kind of cheeky smile. They had something: Lucas knew it in his bones.

"Well," Richie said, "since we've been up, we thought we'd look through CCTV of any hotels, train stations, airports and such to see if we could find that guy."

Andrew smiled in approval; he was liking where this was going.

Richie carried on, "just as we thought, we had a bit of luck." He moved away from the board so the rest of them could see it. There was a screen shot of April's EX, printed out and cello-taped to the board itself with a date and time stamped next to it. Richie pointed to the picture, about to run through their findings. "Here we have him leaving Heathrow three days ago at five in the morning. I checked the CCTV outside the airport and noticed he was picked up in this…" he pointed to a picture of a black Ford Focus that had seen better days. "We kept an eye on CCTV and managed to track it to this location," he pointed at a red cross on a map on the other side of the board. "Now, the only issue we have, is the last we saw on the CCTV is that he arrived at that location which is just twenty-nine miles from here but we don't have an exact address. The location seems to be an array of industrial estates, council houses and blocks of flats. Short of knowing exactly where he is and who he is with, I can't give you more than that. What I can do though is keep a track of the local CCTV to see if we spot him again and I have also sent his name, ID and picture to our connection in the local Police who have him out for arrest as well."

Richie stopped for a second, looking, and probably feeling, quite triumphant. Ethan, Lucas, Jamie, Steve and Andrew were all smiling from ear to ear.

"Did we do good, or did we do good?" Blake asked.

Lucas walked over to the board, quickly scanned through everything they had and smiled again. "You did good boys, really good."

Blake and Richie gave a tacky high five to each other. Ethan rolled his eyes.

"So, where do we go from here?" Ethan asked.

Andrew joined Lucas at the white board while Richie and Blake pulled up a chair each around the table.

"I say we have small teams out on patrol around the area. I also think if we can find that car, we put a tracker on it."

"Good start: I agree Andrew. I also think we need to speak to our connection in the Police to see if he has any records from previous felony's that might help us know some more about him." Lucas replied.

Lucas turned, "Steve, Jamie, can you get four teams of two men, give them all a tracking device, tell them to go to the area and follow what Andrew suggested."

"Anyone in particular Boss?" Steve asked.

"Honestly, for this I don't think we need the best and I would like the Skills Team and The Quad nearby. Anyone who has experience on scouting missions would help."

Steve nodded and then left. Jamie stayed behind.

"You mind if I suggest something?"

"Go on," Lucas encouraged.

"Let me take a car of my own. I'll find out more in an afternoon than a battalion of men."

Lucas stood in thought, though he knew he was going to agree with Jamie anyway. "You're right. Catch up with Steve and tell him what's going on. I still want four teams out though: more eyes the better."

Jamie nodded then left.

"What do you want us to do for the moment?" Andrew questioned.

Lucas's mood soured. "Unfortunately, we have a funeral to plan out."

Ethan slapped the desk next to where he was standing. "Shit, I totally forgot Chris and his team are still here. Do we have the family contacts?"

"Unfortunately, Ethan, we are all the family Chris has. As for the rest, they never gave any next of kin information over when they first joined so I highly doubt there's anyone else we can invite. Truthfully, I think this needs to be just Prevention and low key. The last time we had an event here it didn't exactly go to plan, did it?"

Andrew stopped himself from shouting every swear word in his vocabulary. No: his wedding didn't go to plan at all.

"What do you need from me?" Ethan said, taking a sideways glance at Andrew and keeping his comments to himself. The bloke looked like he was about to blow up.

"Can you speak to Calvin and ask him to get the bodies ready for a service. We'll hold it tomorrow in the afternoon. I also need to ensure the grave sites are ready on the grounds and that everyone knows about it. Richie and Blake, send a general email to everyone stating that Chris and the kitchen team will be having their send-off tomorrow at three thirty. I'll speak to Ellie and Nigel about a buffet and some drinks for the evening wake. Andrew..."

Lucas looked to Andrew and could see the guy was

in his own thoughts. "Andrew..." Lucas said louder. Andrew looked up from his turmoil and raised a brow to Lucas. "Yeah?"

"I'm not going to ask anything of you over the next day or two. I think April will need you more than we will."

"What about tomorrow morning's training for the newbies?"

"Let them have the day off. Lord knows we all need it."

Andrew nodded.

"Blake, Richie, can you arrange the funeral with Calvin please. I also need you both to have your phones and radios on you all the time until this is all over."

They each nodded.

"That's it for the moment then. All I know is I can practically taste the victory on my tongue."

"Just one thing," Andrew started to say, Lucas looked directly at him, "I want to be the one that puts a bullet in his head." He finished his comment and walked out of the room. Ethan was about to go after him but Lucas held him back.

"Leave him. He needs to calm down."

"I get that Boss but that comment gave me chills mate."

"Ethan listen to me, if Andrew can't get his head in the game I need you to step up. That means no more laughing at every, single thing you find funny, it means you taking the lead on certain parts of the operation and when the time comes, if

Andrew freezes or is at risk of putting himself or anyone else in harm, you need to move him and kill April's EX yourself."

Lucas gave Ethan such a harsh look he gulped. He nodded; afraid his voice would let on that the thought of actually having to go over Andrew's head and take his revenge away from him, scared the shit out of him.

CHAPTER 7

Seven drinks down, two large bowls of different cocktails later and April was starting to feel woozy. Since they'd been in the common room, the only topics that had come up were how annoying Ethan was: not that it was something new: how nervous Ellie was about actually having to start her new job role and how Drew was starting to take his first steps. April knew in her heart they wanted to ask her how she was, what was going on with her the last few days and what did she think was going to happen in the future. She knew they wouldn't bring it up though. Though she sat there, had gotten involved in the discussion and tried to fake a constant smile, she knew, as much as they did, that her current situation was a taboo subject.
"So, get this. Ethan comes back late last night, asks me for a blow job then huffs when I tell him to suck it himself because I'm sleeping. Can you believe him?"
Vicky and Amelia laughed, "not to sound patronising Ells but he's a wishful fool. Lucas wouldn't dare wake me up in the middle of a slumber. I'd likely squeeze his balls till they went blue before I agreed

to that."

"I'm so lucky with Steve. He's such a gentleman in bed."

Ellie smirked, "Works well with your prude pants then Vick?" They all burst out laughing, except for April.

"What about Andrew Apes?" Ellie tried to include her in the conversation.

April smiled, "like Steve he's a true gentleman: though not after I've had a drink." She winked at Ellie and downed her eighth cocktail.

"Wheey, go on girl." Amelia laughed and followed suit by downing her drink as well, then both Vicky and Ellie followed.

"April, I haven't wanted to ask but are you *really* ok? You just don't seem yourself?"

April inwardly cringed at Vicky's question. She knew it was coming, still it caught her off guard.

"Truthfully, no I'm not. I let a killer stalk me, marry me, cheat on me and then plan my death. I left him thinking it was all over and he has manged to ruin my life by taking some of the dearest people I know. I feel so guilty all of the time, I don't know what to say to anyone to make it better and I just feel like it's all my fault." Her voiced cracked but she carried on, even as her eyes were filling up with tears. "Why didn't I see this coming? I should have known who and what Matt really was. I lived with him for thirteen years after we got married. How could I have been so fucking dumb to everything."

A lone tear fell from her left eye and she wiped it away. "I'm the reason everyone is dead. I'm the reason my wedding to Andrew was ruined, I'm the reason mum and dad sleep with their alarm on at night. It's me. It's all me and I can't do anything to stop it. I can't make it better." On that last word, April burst out into tears. It was a cry so inconsolable that Ellie, Vicky and Amelia shed tears as well. Ellie moved over to the three-seater where April was, sat down next to her and just held her while she cried. She looked over to Amelia and Vicky and the look on their faces matched Ellie's. They didn't know what to do or say to make April feel any better. Was there anything that would make this better?

Amelia stood up and started pacing around the room. Her look was now furious that someone could have done something like this to one of her friends.

"Look Apes," she said: Ellie let April go so she could look at Amelia.

"If I know our hubbies, which I do, they will know where this prick is and are hunting him down as we speak. They won't let him get away with this."

"He's already won though, hasn't he? One of the Quad has only in the last few days come home from intensive care. He's killed Chris and the kitchen team. He's ruined my wedding day and he's driving a wedge the size of the iceberg that hit the titanic between me and Andrew. All he needs to do to finish off his game is kill Andrew and leave me alive to live with myself. I don't know if I could survive that."

Ellie rubbed April's knee. "I don't think Ethan or Lucas or Steve, would let any harm come to you or Andrew. Plus, let's face it, Andrew is a complete badass! You think Matt will get anywhere near him without Andrew slicing his throat for what he's done to you."

April sniffed back her tears and smiled. "I suppose you're right. He is a badass."

Ellie squeezed April's knee this time. "See, now you're coming round. This building houses more killers than Matt has fingers and toes. The only thing I can see happening in the future is Richie and Blake do their techy thing, they find Matt, Andrew and Lucas will take a task force and kill him in his sleep. We then have a party that the old man is dead, and the world goes back to normal."

"Hear hear," Amelia said as she stopped her pacing and raised an empty glass to the ceiling. "Like, what the hell dudes. We need new drinks to toast this baby into the ground." She gestured to her empty glass with a frown that would put any man to shame.

All the girls laughed at that, including April. April realised as she looked at her sisters and her friend, that this was what she needed. She needed to get things off her chest. She should have said all of these things to Andrew, but she knew he had enough to worry about right now: he had too much to do and too many people, including her, to keep safe.

She stood and raised her own empty glass. "To the kitchen girls for another one of Amelia's, Chernobyl-give-you-webbed-feet-drinks."

"Now you're talking." Vicky said and wrapped her arm around April's waist as they all made a very wobbly way, to the kitchen.

CHAPTER 8

Andrew sat in the kitchen, keeping away from everyone. He didn't trust his own mouth to be pleasant to anyone who spoke to him. He was fuming, utterly incensed to the core. This was coming to a head. He knew he had to think straight else the plan fall through his fingers and Matt gets away, but he just couldn't get his head on right. Matt had to die and he *had* to die by his hand. Only then would he feel he has lived up to April's expectations of keeping her safe, only then would he feel better about all the broken promises he'd made in the past about ending the Hedonists once and for all. Promises he kept on making, that he never intended to break.

Ethan walked into the room and Andrew found himself rolling his eyes. He wasn't in the mood for him right now.

"What you up to muckka?"

"Not a lot Ethan, just considering how much of a failure I am."

"Bah, don't give me that doom and gloom shit. So what some things have gone wrong, so what this has all gone on longer than we thought it would.

We know what's going to happen moving forward, and that's that you will be the big hero on the day, you'll chop this blokes balls off and use them to play tennis, you and blondie will go back to being the envied couple of the century and I can catch a break from Lucas breathing down my neck every five minutes with his 'Ethan you have to do this, Ethan you have to stop laughing, Ethan you must grow up' yadda yadda." Ethan lowered his voice trying to imitate Lucas and even Andrew found himself laughing at the uncanny resemblance.

"You're lucky Lucas wasn't here to hear that. He'd have your guts for garters."

Ethan shrugged, "and then I'd use my charm to make him forgive me."

"Confident much?"

"Gotta be in this day and age mate. Or, I'd end up like you."

Andrew grunted but couldn't stop himself from smiling. He needed this. He needed Ethan's cheeky comments and half-witted responses to lighten the mood in his heart.

"So, where are the gir..." Ethan was cut off mid question. Speak of the Devil and he shall appear.

The four girls walked in completely rat-arsed, singing Bon Jovi's, Living on a Prayer, and Ethan put his hands over his ears before they went to the high key change.

Andrew couldn't help but laugh. Mid chorus the four of them noticed that they weren't alone in the room and went into fits of giggles. Their cheeks were hurting, shoulders shaking and belly's trembling. Someone, not knowing who, even snorted. That made them all laugh even more.

"Was that a cat choir or were my ears deceiving me?" Ethan laughed.

Ellie stuck her tongue out to him and blew him an unladylike raspberry. "Boo you: you couldn't sing this song if your dick was caught in your zip."

All the girls looked at each other, and another outburst of laughs sounded around the kitchen and bounced off the white walls.

Ethan looked at Andrew. "I am not looking forward to tonight. If she yaks, she's coming to your room mate."

Andrew smiled, "contrary to what you think, I am very much looking forward to tonight." He winked at April and she felt her cheeks blush. Everyone knew how frisky the sisters got with some alcohol in their system. Steve, Andrew and Ethan had a challenge on their hands come bedtime.

"So, not to put a downer on your day girls but who's going to be doing lunch? Obviously, *you're* in no fit state Ells."

She flippantly waved her hand in the air at Ethan. "Nig is doing it today. He'll be here soon so get off my back mush."

Ethan shook his head: he really wasn't looking forward to tonight.

"What are you all doing anyway? Asides from bringing the house down with your signing?" Andrew asked them all.

In synchronicity they each held up their empty glasses. They were here for a top up then.

Andrew laughed. "Maybe go back to the common room and I'll bring some bits in to you. I would imagine the cleaners don't want extra work by cleaning the spillage of your drinks from the carpet."

"Sounds like a plan batman." Amelia followed her comment by putting her glass on one of the tables closest to the door. The other three followed her actions and they all turned to leave. The moment they were out of sight they heard Amelia say, "what about Guns and Roses?" Vicky piped in, "oh I looooovvveeee Sweet Child of Mine." Then as predictable as the sun coming up in the morning and setting in the evening, their wails of voices started singing their next classic Rock song.

As soon as they were completely out of sight, Ethan turned to Andrew. "Would you have married April knowing her voice is as bad as tyres screeching on the road?"

Andrew laughed, "I'd have married her if she had no voice at all Ethan."

Ethan rolled his eyes, "soppy bollocks, but to be fair, when they're like this, it does make me smile. Nothing like a bit of oestrogen in a building full of testosterone!"

Andrew stood, "you're quite right. What have you got on today?"

"Honestly, keeping you company mate. Steve is off doing his thing, Jamie is about to leave to do his thing, Richie, Blake and Lucas are arranging the funeral for tomorrow with Calvin and I'm on small dick duty."

"I guess that starts with more alcohol for the misses then," Andrew shrugged, picked up all the glasses from the table and headed into the kitchen. Just as he did, Nigel and a few others arrived.

"I take it that godawful sound is the four of them drunk?" Nigel said to Ethan.

Ethan laughed, "yep, I'm afraid you guys are on your own this lunch time. You ain't getting any help from Ellie whatsoever."

Nigel's look of concern was as evident as Ethan's look of amusement.

"Nig, what we going to do?" his small team asked behind him: looking as concerned as he was.

"I reckon we can probably get away with salad, chicken and potatoes. Easy to do but also good for the weather?"

All of them looked relieved. There was nothing easier than cutting things up and putting them in dishes without having to actually cook each item separately.

All of them got to work, just as Andrew was coming out of the back room with a bowl of red, iced liquid and four clean glasses balanced precariously under his chin. Nigel raised a brow at him, carried on tying his apron round his waist and said nothing.

"Let me grab those." Ethan came over and took the glasses from under Andrew's chin. They headed to the common room where the chorus of ACDC's

Back in Black was being belted by the girls.

Ethan looked to Andrew before they got in the room. "I don't know about you, but I ain't staying here and being a part of this. Wanna go to the gym after?"

Andrew nodded. "That'd be good."

As they rounded the corner to the living room, Ethan wiped a hand down his face and Andrew couldn't help but laugh. In the midst of their private karaoke, they had moved all the red chesterfield sofa's to the side of the room, Amelia was in the corner next to a table, trying to connect her phone Bluetooth to the stereo system and the rest of them were dancing and singing like they didn't have a care in the world.

It took a moment for them to notice Andrew and Ethan at the door and when they did, they cheered like a group of Sailors on leave. Andrew walked in and placed the punch bowl on the table next to Amelia, Ethan left the glasses next to that and they made a quick escape before they too, were dragged in to this shenanigan of day drinking, dancing and singing.

CHAPTER 9

William received Jo's text about an hour ago. He did not want to go anywhere near Jo's right now as he knew Matt would be there. To say William was in the doghouse would be the understatement of the century. Not only did his plan fail to kill April and the other guys with the bomb he was meant to have set up properly, but he'd been avoiding everyone in the Hedonist group since he walked away from the warehouse that day they took April's sister. He didn't even get involved in storming the wedding: he'd avoided that like a bad hangover. It was all too much for him. How many times over the last few weeks had he contemplated going to the Police and telling them everything, how many times he'd visited his brothers grave and had been so close to going to that compound and telling April and her crew everything they needed to know to stop all of this. How many more people had to die? His brother had already paid the price of someone else's revenge with his life.

He bit his lip and a shudder went through him as he stood at the bottom of the apartment complex with his finger near the buzzer for Jo's floor.

It wasn't a shudder from the cold breeze, it wasn't a shudder from the iced latte he had on the way here, it was a shudder from fear and dread. What despicable thing were they trying to get him to do now: what else would Matt try to do to see his Ex-wife in the ground.

William took a breath, then pressed the buzzer. The tannoy on the machine next to the floor buttons screeched before William heard Jo. "Is that you mouse?"

William grit his teeth. "Yeah, it's me."

The tannoy cut off and the door to the building was buzzed open. William walked in and the smell of stale urine and cannabis hit him hard. Each floor had five different apartments on it and it was seven storeys high. The worst of the worst lived here. It felt more like a prison than a block of flats.

William reached Jo's and hesitated before he knocked. Jo must have known he was there. As William's hand was about to reach for the door, Jo opened it up with a furious look on his face.

"What's up with you?" William asked.

"You try having that arsehole living with you and then tell me you'll look any different to what I do now." Jo moved out of the way so William could enter. William didn't say a word. As hot-headed as Jo was on the calmest of days, any fuel to add to the fire would be dangerous for William. He didn't want his head caved in from Mr Steroid.

William sheepishly walked through Jo's hallway, expecting Matt to be in the living room, sat down developing some master plan that would see them all dead, but instead, the room was empty. William took a breath of relief and took a seat.

Jo walked in and sat down as well.

"Nice place you got here." William said. Lying through his teeth. It wasn't nice at all. It was small, grimy, everything was painted white and the furniture had seen better days.

"Yeah right. Even I know you're lying. This place is a dive." Jo shrugged his shoulders.

"Where is he?"

"Hopefully get hitting by a car somewhere."

William laughed at that. Maybe Jo was starting to feel the same as he was, that all of this was just pointless. Futile.

"I think he's gone over to one of the vacant warehouses down the road. He's looking for a place to lure her out and kill her and her fella."

"How is he going to lure her out?"

"The idiot wants me to act as if I've left the Hedonists, to take a message to that compound and tell them where he's going to be. He thinks they'll believe me."

"They might do." Though as William said it, he doubted they would. They would likely shoot him on site than take him in for a chat and a cuppa.

"Give over will you. They won't take anything I say as truth. One of them saw me you know. That day Malcolm was taken, one of them saw me. I tried to stop it but Malcolm was hit over the head and knocked out. If I go anywhere near that building,

I'll be dead before I can open my mouth. But you…"
Jo let his comment trail off as he knew William was in for a much better chance at surviving than he was.

"Forget it. I'm not going anywhere near there. You're lucky I came here today."

Jo lowered his eyes at William. "You'll do as you're told mouse. You, they don't know. You seem like a little weasel they would believe to have left us and are betraying us."

"Jo I don't want to go. I want out."

Jo was about to put his foot down but the main door intercom sounded out through his apartment.

"That'll be him." He got up to let Matt in and William wished he'd never come here. He hasn't seen *him* for a while. This was about to change William's life for the worse.

William sat, nervously biting his lip right up until the moment Matt walked into Jo's front room and gave him a glare so evil William gulped.

"Still alive then?" Matt said.

William nodded. He didn't say anything for fear his voice would betray him and show just how frightened he was.

"And to what do we owe the pleasure?" Matt said, while taking the last seat on the sofa: too close to William for his liking.

"Jo text me and asked me to come over."

Matt looked at Jo who was sitting in his single chair by the laptop desk. "Why?"

Jo shrugged, "haven't seen him for a while. I also thought he could deliver the message."

A look of acknowledgment passed Matt's eyes. "I like your thinking Jo. *You*, they'll believe." He looked at William with a grin that would make a baby cry.

William gulped again, seriously regretting answering Jo's message.

"I've set up the meeting point. I know the message. You just need to get close enough to her to deliver it."

"And how am I meant to do that?" William asked.

"I'm sure Jo will fill you in if he hasn't already. I need a shower." And without even asking, he got up and went to use Jo's facilities as if he were paying for it all himself.

William looked at Jo and could practically see the fire in his eyes. Once they both heard the loud hum of water hitting the bottom of the bathtub, Jo moved closer to William.

"You *will* do this. You'll go to the compound, tell them his message and plan but at the same time, we're going to set him up. I've had enough of his shit to last me a lifetime and the sooner he's gone, the sooner we can all move on."

CHAPTER 10

The day had gone quicker than Lucas wanted it to. Lunch and dinner were a complete mess, no, a catastrophe of epic proportions. The sooner Ellie's hand got better and the sooner her and all the women sobered up, the better.

He sat with his head in his hands in the tech lab, waiting for Jamie to return.

"You ok Boss?"

Lucas looked up at Richie. "Yeah, I'm ok, just a lot to do and not enough time. Is everything ready for tomorrow?"

"Yeah, it is and I've ordered a catering company to come and sort out the buffet for the wake. I didn't want to go over your head and use some of the budget without asking you, but I really don't think Ellie will be in a fit state to sort it out and after today's escapades with Nigel and the lunch and dinner, I thought it'd be best to get some professional help."

Lucas smiled. "Thank you. It was the right thing to do. Has everyone actioned the email and replied their receipt of the funeral?"

"Everyone apart from us, you, the ladies and Jamie.

He probably hasn't got his emails linked to his phone yet. Though I guarantee he'll be coming."

Lucas nodded in agreement.

"Here he is." Blake said as Jamie walked in through the tech lab door.

"Been waiting long?" Jamie asked them all.

"No, though with the day I've had it feels like a lifetime."

"Dare I ask?"

"All I'm going to say is you should thank your luck you weren't here today. Ellie, April, Amelia and Vicky got so drunk they are all in their rooms throwing up. Nigel and his team managed to bugger up lunch and dinner. I mean, who the hell can get salad wrong?"

Jamie laughed, "ahh, the art of chopping up lettuce. It's a skill."

Lucas gave a huff of a laugh, "I tell you; the sooner things go back to normal the better. I can't take another day of sorting out the kitchen, arranging funerals and keeping on top of the new recruits. Anyway, did you have a better day?"

Jamie sat down, two seats away from Lucas. "Actually, I did. I found that car. It's parked outside an apartment complex that makes Alcatraz look like a holiday camp. There are a few warehouses around the estate which I think will be good for some teams to hold up and recon. I put a tracker on the car as well."

Lucas smiled as he felt a wave of delight go through him. This was good news. Like a bad chapter in a poorly written book, this was soon to be over and forgotten about. Lucas only hoped that on the day, whenever that may be, Andrew pulls himself together and is able to do what he needs to do. For Andrews sake, Lucas hopes he's able to bring himself back from the denial he's surfing right now.

"What tracker number was it?" Richie asked Jamie. Jamie pulled the small, empty box out of his back pocket and handed it over. Within minutes, Richie had the tracker on his screen. He made it mirror on one of the projectors and Lucas looked over his shoulder. A red blinking dot on a map signalled the route to everyone's problems but also, the solution that may get them all out of this.

"Blake and Richie, I want you to keep an eye on that car like a hawk. Also, keep an eye on the Hedonists APP. I have a funny feeling they may want to cause havoc as they execute their plan and I will not have an auction affecting everyone's ability to get the job done."

They nodded as Lucas stood. He went over to the building tannoy on Blakes desk. After switching on the button and waiting for the interference to stop, Lucas put the speaker to his mouth. "All Prevention Soldier's report to the gym. I repeat, all Prevention Soldier's to report to the gym."

"You want company?" Jamie asked as Lucas finished his message to the building.

"I do, I also want you to take the lead on some of this."

"Right you are Boss."

They both left to head to the gym. Jamie hadn't before seen the building when it was like this. Every Solider, all in their ranking colours of blue, were headed to the gym in teams. Jamie was quite impressed by the discipline of everyone. Lucas said 'do something' and everyone followed without a word.

As they were walking down the stairs, Andrew and Ethan came out of the hallway to Andrew's room.

"Everyone ok Lucas?"

"Yes Andrew, though I could ask you both the same? How's drunken one and drunken two?"

"Ha, don't ask. Ells and April are currently taking it in turns holding each other's hair back while the other one voms all over small dick's clean toilet here. Thank god they didn't come back to my room." Ethan answered for him, and Andrew shrugged.

"He's right. They really are emptying their stomachs like they have food poisoning. So, what's with the meeting at the gym?"

"I need to address everyone together. We've got a lead. I also need them to be aware of tomorrow's funeral. I don't want anything going wrong."

Andrew nodded and followed Jamie and Lucas to the gym, with Ethan tailing the rear. All four of them were wearing black, as their leader colours denote, and a few newbies stopped to look at them in admiration. They looked like a swat team ready for battle. Something to aspire to I would imagine.

The four leaders stood just left of the gym doors, waiting for everyone to filter in. Once the last few stragglers entered, Lucas turned on the ceiling lights to the olive-green painted gymnasium. He headed for the stage with Andrew, Ethan and Jamie following him.

He stood as the focal point on the podium, facing his team of trained killers. Four rows of blue camouflaged men stood to face him. It was easy to spot the new recruits. They all looked smaller and were nervous: Lucas could tell by the way their eyes were darting around the other men, not focusing on any one person longer than a few seconds.

"Prevention, we have a lot to discuss here today. By now, anyone not new to us will know that we've had a bad rift with the Hedonist's lately. Since their leaders were killed and we found out April was their main target, we've not had much luck in finding out who was behind everything and why. We now know that April's EX husband is the last remaining leader. He is the reason things have been going the way they have recently. We still don't know why but that's a discussion for another day." Lucas stopped for a second to let this news sink in. He could see three of the Quad looking enraged beyond sane at what they heard, the Special Skills Team looked just as furious. They had lost good men and nearly lost Scott from the Quad, on April's past lover. Lucas looked to Colin from the Skills Team then to Tom and Craig from the Quad. They nodded and he carried on.

"In the last day we have found out a potential location of where the last leader may be and the last members of the Hedonists who are still loyal to him. For the record, his name is Matt. What we know is his connections go back to the very first leaders. He was involved in the setting up and the creating of the Hedonists and April was always going to be a target for auction. Things changed and April ended up married to him longer than intended. We do not know why, but again, that is a discussion for another day. Moving forward, we must plan this out effectively. Meaning, he dies, and none of us get caught in the crossfire. Jamie, can I ask you to take over for a second." Lucas looked to his right and nodded at Jamie; Jamie stepped forward to address the room.

"The location of a car that has been involved, is in the industrial and housing estate in Ramsgate. I've been there today and put a tracker on the car in question. The main building I think he's located in, is a rundown apartment block that's seven storey's high. There's two ways in and out. The main front of the building has intercom for each flat so people are buzzed in, and there's a fire escape round the back. There are three warehouses near the block of flats, and all have keen vantage points for scout's recon. I say we hold up in the buildings in teams for a while and play this safe. I wouldn't want to risk us going in too early and being found out. We need to do this covertly and stealthily if we're to have a chance at killing this guy."

Jamie took a step back and Lucas took the stage again.

"Over the next few days, Andrew and Ethan will be working with some of you on what your roles will be in this moving forward. As you can imagine, not everyone will be needed for this so New Recruits, you're staying here for the foreseeable future. I'll also need some help from you all tomorrow. I am sure by now you have seen the email about Chris, Tony and Simon's funerals. Need I say this will be a difficult day for us all. More pointedly is that the last time we held an event here, the Hedonists managed to scout the building, get in and kill the kitchen team and ruin Andrew and April's wedding day. I need about twelve volunteers to patrol the grounds at all times. That's it for now, we'll meet here at nine a.m. sharp tomorrow morning to clarify who is doing what. If you want to volunteer, I suggest you stand to the left in the morning. Everyone, be aware that this will not be easy. Dismissed."

The mood of the room and all of his Soldier's hung in the air like a cloud of despair and fear that was fusing with anger and rage. Too many times they had planned missions to end this, too many times had things gone wrong, too many times had Prevention lost. Lucas knew it in his bones that this was the end game. By the end of this, one of two things would have happened: either Prevention wins, or they do. There is no middle ground here. There are no half measures to take. They go in for the kill or be killed. It was as simple as that.

Lucas turned to the leaders on the stage as the room emptied. Once they were on their own he put a hand on Andrew's shoulder.

"You've been quiet."

"I don't know what to say Lucas. I want him dead. I want to know he is in the ground with maggots eating his eyes and that April never has to worry about him again."

Lucas smiled, "bit morbid but I get what you mean. This *will* all finish Andrew."

"To what end though Lucas? Theirs or ours? I can't stop thinking about what will happen if they manage to kill her. I would have failed Lucas. I would have failed so severely my life wouldn't be worth living."

Jamie stepped closer, "you're thinking about this all wrong. We can take the lead on this. We *will* kill him Andrew."

"He needs to die by my hand." Andrew wriggled himself out from under Lucas's hand and walked out of the room. Ethan went to go after him but Lucas stopped him.

"Let him be. Nothing we say right now will make him feel any better about this. Ethan, Jamie I need you to look after him over the next few days. When you plan something, tell him: when we have some new intel, tell him."

Jamie nodded. Ethan still stood in the same position since Andrew walked out of the room.

"Boss I hate this. Andrew can't be this affected by

all of this. I mean, Silvia was serious and I knew how badly he coped with the guilt but it's like he's given up trying. He's writing April off as dead before we can work out a full proof plan to end it all."

"I know Ethan. Honestly, I haven't seen Andrew like this since his EX left him. Nothing good can come from his attitude right now."

"Agreed." Jamie added. "We'll get through tomorrow and do the best we can for him. If we have to, we'll set it up so perfectly that Andrew deals the blow. I have a funny feeling it'll give him the retribution he's craving."

Lucas nodded in agreement. "Look, go and get your heads down for the night. Ethan tell Ellie that Richie and Blake have organised caterers for the wake tomorrow so she can relax without having to worry. Jamie, reach out to Steve for me and feedback what happened with his teams today and what they found out. Chances are, they don't know any more than we do right now but it'll be good to know what went on."

"See you laters taters," Ethan said, as he jumped off the stage and ran after Andrew.

"Till the morning Boss. If you need me, just shout out." Jamie then turned to leave as well, leaving only Lucas to drown in his thoughts for a little while longer.

CHAPTER 11

Ethan managed to get to Andrew, just as he was about to open the door to his room.

"Sup small dick?"

"Not now Ethan. I really haven't got the patience for you right now."

Ethan held his hands up, palms facing Andrew as if to say 'ok, I'll leave it.' "I'm only here to grab Ellie the drunken bum."

Andrew couldn't stop the half smile that played on the edges of his mouth. Now Ethan knew he was breaking down Andrew's wall, he put his arm around him and pulled him in to him. Andrew struggled to get out from Ethan's grip but his hold was vice tight.

"Will you bloody let me go!"

"Na, not yet. You need this bro; you need a cuddle and some man love. I can tell you're sinking in despair right now and I need you to let it all out. Breathe small dick, breathe." As Ethan said this, he persisted on squeezing Andrews shoulders in a massive bear hug and showing him how to take deep breaths.

Andrew rolled his eyes. "I don't need to breathe

you dickhead, I need to kill that bastard, I need to live up to the expectations April has of me to protect her and keep her safe, and I need to fucking sleep."

Ethan let him go but took Andrew's hands in his. Andrew looked down at their interlocked fingers and raised his eyebrows to Ethan.

"Look small dick…"

"Stop with the fucking small dick will you. I know what you're trying to do and it isn't helping."

"Shhhh shhhh shhhh…. It will help if you let it. Mate you have to let go of all this anger, if not, you ain't going to win. How many times have you told Blondie to let it go? All the times she'd spent crying, not eating and sleeping she was letting him win, wasn't she? Sound familiar to you?"

Andrew continued to look at his own hands in Ethan's. He didn't want to admit it, but Ethan was right. He'd given enough advice over the last year or so, maybe it was about time he started taking some of it.

"I know. I just can't. Put yourself in my shoes. I'm failing Ethan. I'm failing as a leader; I'm failing as a Husband and I'm failing as a man."

Just as Andrew finished what he was saying, the door to his room opened and April stood there wrapped in a black dressing gown, with her wet hair in a towel. Her face was bare of makeup but that didn't diminish her natural beauty. Her lips were full and pink, her face was glowing and her blue eyes twinkled behind the tears.

Andrew quickly pulled his hands out of Ethan's. Not that April noticed. Her eyes had been focused so intently on Andrews face she wouldn't have noticed if they were wearing tutus and ballet slippers.

"You are not failing me or anyone else. You listen to me, you've protected me, you helped save Ellie from their clutches, you saved me more times than I can remember, and you've done right by your team here. Eliminate those thoughts from your mind right away. You are the best thing that has ever happened to me, and I would be completely lost without you." She gave a shy smile.

Ethan looked at her approvingly. *That* was exactly what Andrew needed to hear.

Devoid of a second to think about what he was doing, Andrew stepped straight up to April and lifted her in his arms. The kiss they had would have given the Notebook's kiss a run for its money. April's hands flew to cradle Andrew's face, their lips were connected in such a way Ethan was sure they couldn't breathe: the only thing it was missing was fireworks.

Ethan looked past them to see Ellie stood by the bathroom door with her jaw dropped. "Ells it's time to go babe. I think I know where this is heading, and you better believe I ain't staying here to see Andrew's small dick in action mate."

Ellie looked at Ethan, picked up her chin from the floor and grabbed her tennis shoes. She walked past April and Andrew and didn't say a word. She didn't want to ruin any moment between them. They needed this. They needed to get back to themselves and show each other just how much they loved one and another.

Ellie shut the door as she left. Ethan was about to pick her up in a fireman carry but she moved out of his grip. "Don't babe, I'll throw up if you touch me."

He laughed, "you actually been puking the whole time since we left earlier?"

"Yeah, though now it's nothing but dry heaving."

"Well, you will do this to yourself. Drink to oblivion then waste it all by letting it hit the royal chamber pot."

She looked at him and frowned.

"Just get me to bed will you."

He took her shoes from her hand and grabbed hold of the other one and led her to their room.

"By the way, we've got caterers for the wake tomorrow. Lucas is giving you a day off."

"Well thank ye kindly Mr Boss man."

Ethan laughed as they finished their walk to their room. Ethan hated feeling like this, but his back was up and his nerves were shot to oblivion. This had to work out. It just had to!

CHAPTER 12

Amelia rolled over and groaned when she realised she was alone in her bed. Drew was crying and she did *not* have the energy to be without Lucas this morning. She pulled herself out of bed, well, rolled herself out of bed, didn't care that she was in nothing but her birthday suit as walked to Drew's room. She stopped at the door and felt her heart melt in her chest. Lucas was cradling Drew is his arms, trying to get him to calm down with a bottle of milk. Drew was old enough now to hold his drink so he took it from Lucas's hands and started sucking on the teat. Amelia smiled as Lucas gave such a tender kiss to Drew's head while he was swaying him from side to side. Amelia would never get tired of seeing her strong and reliable husband go weak at the knees for their boy.

Lucas turned around and saw her leaning against the door frame.

He smiled. "Sorry love, I didn't want to wake you." She walked over to him and put her arms around his waist and rested her head on Drew's. "I love seeing you like this and being in this room. It reminds me there is still, some normality in our lives."

"Little piece of heaven in a world full of hell." He responded and kissed her cheek.

"You might want to shower and start getting ready love. I have to meet the Soldier's in the gym at nine."

She kissed his lips, savouring the feel of butterflies that he always gave her, and headed to shower and get ready.

Drew pulled the bottle away from his mouth and started wriggling in Lucas's arms. He put him down in his play pen and turned on the TV to the kid's channel. He sat on the chair in Drew's room and took a moment to look around. Amelia was right. Being in this room was a small touch of normality. Drew's room was painted light blue on one wall that had art work of clouds and the sun on it, his small crib was to the left of the room by the window and his playpen was next to that. Drew sat there smashing building blocks together and squealing in delight. Lucas smiled. Drew didn't have a single clue how loved he was.

Lucas's phone started vibrating in his left pocket. Normality was evidently about to come to an end. He took it out and saw Andrew's name light up.

"Andrew, everything ok?"

"Yeah Lucas. Everything is ok. I called as I just wanted to apologise for the way I've been acting the last few days."

"Say no more my friend. I know it's been hard for you and I understand why. What's brought this on? I haven't heard you apologise to another man since you threw Roger three feet in the air and broke his arm."

Andrew laughed, "I know. Idiot shouldn't have gotten in my way should he, though I did feel bad the next day seeing him in a cast. Probably didn't make matters better for him when Ethan drew a massive cock on it in bright pink marker pen."

Lucas actually laughed out loud at that. "God that was funny. So how are you?"

"Honestly, better mate. I had a good conversation with April last night who made me realise a few things."

"Such as?"

"That I can't do this on my own and I've done nothing to make her think any less of me."

"You haven't and you can't. She's right you know. I know you feel like everything you touch right now is turning to dogshit but it's unchartered ground mate. We'd all be the same."

"I know, I was also lucky enough to have some of Ethan's, free therapy last night as well."

Again, Lucas laughed, "tell me."

"The idiot cuddled me while telling me I needed to let go of my anger and then persisted to try and get me to do relaxing breathing techniques. He then took my hands as if he were about to propose and gave me some hard truths."

Lucas couldn't stop laughing.

"Yeah, yeah ok, jokes over." Andrew joined Lucas and started laughing as well. Why Ethan was such a child was beyond them, but he definitely made

every situation a little better, just by being himself.
"I'm sorry Andrew but I can picture your face the moment he took your hands." Lucas carried on laughing.
"If looks could kill we'd be having *his* funeral today." Andrew carried on laughing as well.
"Something funny?"
Lucas looked to the door where Amelia was stood in a towel. Her long brown hair was hanging down past her shoulders and her grey eyes were somehow smiling to match her mouth.
"No love, just Ethan trying to therapize Andrew."
She waved her hand in the air as she walked away. She didn't need to know. Only to ask what he had done this time would damage one of her brain cells with his stupidity.
"Sorry about that Andrew."
"It's fine. So, is everything planned for today?"
"As planned as it can be. I've had Richie and Blake check the credentials of the caterers. We know who is coming, have their pictures as well so anyone not already known will not be coming in the grounds. I've got to address the team in an hour, but we'll set up armed patrols, I've got Blake and Richie with radio's, Calvin is on standby should anything go wrong and I'm delivering the service."
"Ok. Look mate I'm sorry you've had to plan this on your own."
"There's nothing to it. I don't want to hear any more dwelling ok. I'll see you in the gym at nine."
"Will do. Thanks again Lucas."

"Any time mate, any time."

Andrew hung up and Lucas checked his phone. Since he'd been on the call with Andrew he'd had a few missed calls from the Tech Lab. He dialled the number.

"Sorry to call you so early Boss."

"It's fine Blake, what's the matter?"

"That car has moved. We're currently tracking it but my gut is telling me it's on its way here?"

"Here? Now?"

"Yeah. It's taking the main A roads to get to the grounds of the camp. It'll be here within the next two hours."

Lucas could have howled over the phone. He could have thrown the phone at the wall. Why, of all the days did they have to make their move now.

"Boss?" Blake questioned as Lucas had been quiet for too long.

"Yeah, I'm here. I'm on my way. Oh, and Blake, don't lose that fucking car."

"You got it." Blake hung up.

Lucas took a moment to calm down. He needed a clear head for this. Why were they coming to the compound? Were they really that stupid? How did they think they were going to get anywhere near the building? Something was going on. Something wasn't going to plan. It was their plan, he hoped, that was the one failing.

He called Andrew back, he answered on the third ring. "You ok?"

"Can you meet me at the tech lab in ten minutes?"

"Sure, why though?"

"That car is currently on its way here."

"That car? *His* fucking car you mean?"

"Well, the car that was known to have picked him up, yes. I have a feeling this is either part of his plan or something is about to go very wrong for him."

"I'll be there in five." Andrew hung up.

Lucas quickly ran to his bedroom and got dressed in his black, leadership uniform. Amelia looked at him as he was getting ready.

"Tell me everything is ok?"

He walked over to her and took both her hands in his. "It is and if it isn't, it will be." He planted a kiss on her lips, grabbed his phone off the bed and left. He heard Amelia shout out "cryptic" as he shut their door.

CHAPTER 13

Matt had requested that Jo text William to meet them at Jo's apartment. It was seven in the morning and if William didn't turn up in the next few minutes, he'd turn up fucking dead. Matt didn't have the tolerance for this today.

He was about to stand up and start pacing the floor in Jo's front room when the buzzer sounded for the door. Jo got up and let William in. A few minutes later, William walked through the door looking as though he could cry at any minute.

"What took you so long?"

"I don't live that close and there was traffic."

"Traffic? You're blaming this on traffic?"

William looked at Jo, desperately wishing that if he lashes out, Jo stops him.

"Sorry."

"Keep your sorry's to yourself you wimp. I have to get that message to her today. You need to take Jo's car, head to that compound and demand to be let in. You will ask to speak with Andrew and April and no one else. You hear me: no one else."

William felt the saliva try and slip down his dry throat. He was petrified. He either did as Matt asked and got a beating from her fella and his crew, or he didn't do as Matt asked and Matt kills him on the spot. It was a lose, lose situation. The mother of all ultimatums.

He nodded.

"You're to tell them that you've had enough of being a part of the Hedonists group. That you heard about another member of the team taking a message to them and you had to get to them first. You'll say you heard me tell this other person that they *have* to meet me in the warehouse directly in front of this building tomorrow morning before the sun rises. If they are not on their own I'll blow up the building with everyone in it."

"What if they say no: what if they don't believe me."

"They will and you know why, because you'll tell them you heard me say that if they don't come, that I will kill her parents, I'll kill his parents and every single person they know outside of that facility if they don't."

"And what are you going to do when they get there."

The look that passed Matt's features was truly something of horror. That look right there is what birthed an entire genre of nightmares. Instinctively, William took a step closer to Jo.

"I'm going to haul up on the top floor. They'll bring a team with them, they won't be able to fucking help themselves. I'm going to wait until her and that waste of oxygen walk through the doors at the front, then I'm going to set off an explosion blocking them in and the others out. Nothing too big. Just enough to stop anyone getting past the rubble quickly. I'm then going to call her upstairs by using an old nickname I had for her when we were married and pounce. I'm going to kill him with my bare hands in front of her and when I've finished, I'm going to take this gun..." he stopped to take the small revolver out from his belt loop at the back and show case his weapon of choice, "and I'm going to put it right here on her face..." he walked over to William to place the barrel of the gun in between his eyebrows... "and I'm going to pull the fucking trigger and watch as her brains fly out of the back of her head as she dies once and for all."

William was beside himself with fear. This man was deranged. He was evil personified. He had to be stopped.

Matt pulled the gun away from Williams face and put it back in its place: in his belt loop, flush with his back, just waiting to be used.

"One last thing before you go mouse..." William turned to see what Jo wanted. He shouldn't have. *That* should have been his moment to run. He didn't though, he wasn't brave enough. He simply stood there in shock as Jo grabbed him by the scruff of the neck and held him in place: an easy target for Matt's punches. Blow after blow landed on his eyes, his nose, his ribs and his groin.

Once Matt finished, Jo let him go and William fell to the ground in agony. He couldn't see past the blood in his eyes, couldn't taste anything but the salty flavour of his blood in his mouth and couldn't smell anything past the blood bouquet in his nose. He whimpered.

Matt bent down and handed him a small wet tea towel. "Now they'll believe you're against us."

CHAPTER 14

Andrew, Jamie, Tom and Craig were currently walking down to the gates of Preventions grounds. It left only Lucas and Ethan to brief the rest of the team on what was happening and why today must go to plan. Chris and his team must be laid to rest. Everyone needed the closure and Andrew didn't want to admit it, but by the time the week was done, he feared they'd also need the room in the morgue.

If they timed this right, that car should be at the gates in roughly twenty minutes. All four of them were armed, all four of them had radio's, trackers and bullet proof jackets: all four of them were prepared to die to stop this car getting anywhere near the building.

"It's a bold move I'll give them that."

"Bold my arse," Andrew replied to Jamie. "Something's amiss with this and I want to know what their game is." He finished his bitter comment and started walking up and down the big, gated fence. The fence itself at the bottom of the compound ran almost the entire length of the grounds. Eight feet tall and topped with barbwire, no one would get past it. April had been one of the unlucky ones that managed to get to the facility all those years ago by veering off the A roads near her town. It was the only way into the compound through the fence, and the only reason it didn't have a fence was because the local council thought it would draw attention if it was easily seen from daily traffic.

As Andrew was pacing and huffing to himself, Jamie looked at Tom and Craig. Knowing Nigel was the last member of The Quad, he totally got their name. He hadn't met Scott yet who was still recovering from his injuries, but if he looked anything like the others, he knew the name was fitting. All of them had blonde hair usually gelled in quiffs: long, trimmed blonde beards and the thousand-yard stare. Both Tom and Craig shrugged their shoulders at Andrew's comment. In no words, it said they completely agreed with Andrew and were as bitter about this as he was.

Ten minutes passed and Andrew had continued his pacing. He kept looking down one end of the road to the other and checking the L85 Rifle he had in his hand: he was cursing everything and everyone under his breath.

At last they had movement on the road. As soon as Andrew heard the car coming up the hill he signalled the three of them to fall behind. He stood behind the gate and peered through the gap in the fence. With his hand in the air, fingers up, waiting to drop it and have them all filter out, he paused when the car pulled up.

The Ford Focus had definitely seen better days. The black paint was fading, there was a dent in the bumper on the driver side rear and the windscreen was cracked: it was even sporting a spare tyre. How it passed any vehicle safety checks was a mystery. More than the state of the car was the state of the driver. As soon as the car came to a stop the driver door opened and a small, mousey looking guy fell out of it. He lie there on the floor, barely moving but it was obvious why. His face was covered in blood and bruises, he was bent over in such a way Andrew knew his ribs were possibly broken and he may have internal bleeding. How he managed to drive here was more than questionable.

Andrew turned around and looked at Jamie. His face said it all. *This*, they weren't expecting.

"Move out," Andrew said, and the three of them moved in synchronisation to flank him. Andrew pressed the button on the gate for it to swing open and all of them had their gun sights lined up to their eyes.

"Keep an eye on the area. This could be a trap." Jamie said.

Andrew walked over to the guy on the floor and nudged his shoulder with his foot. The guy groaned.

"Oi, what happened to you? Why are you here?" Andrew asked and to his utter astonishment, the guy started crying.

Andrew looked at Jamie, mystified.

"Andrew…"

The guy's voice was so quiet Andrew had to get down on his knees and closer to his mouth to hear what he'd said.

"What was that?"

"Andrew?"

"Yeah, I'm Andrew: why do you want to know?"

"Help... me..." the guy's voice trailed off and he passed out.

Andrew didn't know what to do. He didn't expect this. It didn't make sense.

He looked at Jamie. "Well, I'm stumped."

Jamie laughed, "I have a feeling he was sent to send a message. I think it rings loud and clear that this guy is at the bottom of the pecking order. I'll radio Lucas."

Jamie walked off and started speaking into his radio.

He came back seconds later. "Get him in the car and we'll drive it up to the camp. I'm going to check the car for any bombs or anything first though, don't need that causing a scene on the day of the funeral's, do we?"

Jamie nodded to Craig and Tom. The three of them checked the vehicle over with the finest of toothcombs and only when they were satisfied it was clear, did they pick the guy up with Andrew and get him in the back. There wasn't enough room for all of them, so Andrew drove it back up to the facility building, Jamie sat in the passenger seat which left Tom and Craig to walk.

Just before Andrew started the car he looked to

Tom and Craig. "You ok walking back?"

"Yeah, need to get my steps up anyway." Craig said.

Tom rolled his eyes. "Fitness freak strikes again."

Andrew laughed and pulled off. He checked the rear-view mirror and saw Tom shut the gate before both of them started their incline up the hill.

"What did Lucas say?"

"Exactly what I thought Andrew, that this guy was sent to send a message. Lucas wants him taken to the med lab. He's going to ask a few of the Special's to keep an eye on him until he's ready to talk. Calvin is on standby already."

"Hopefully he starts talking before three thirty, I can't let April stand at that funeral on her own."

"You won't have to. I can miss it if I need to. I didn't know Chris and his team as well as you guys. It's the least I can do."

Andrew smiled. Lucas had made the right decision by offering Jamie a full-time role. He was integral to the team, integral to the entire operation.

CHAPTER 15

April was feeling like she'd been hit by the hangover branch this morning. Not only was her head hurting from all the boose yesterday, her legs were hurting from the quite, unnatural positions Andrew had her in last night and her stomach muscles ached from the vomiting as well. Why oh why did she do this to herself? She should know by now that she can't drink as much as she used to. Back when she was on the larger side of flattering, she'd been able to keep up with the best of them. She used to tell herself that all the extra fat helped soak up the alcohol. Now she was slimmer the alcohol went straight to her head and out from her gut and bladder.

At least one good thing came from last night, and that was her and Andrew talking things out. The reassurance she gave him seemed to ignite his fire again and he seemed like the man she fell in love with. Strong, kind, just. Even though something was wrong this morning when she heard Lucas call him back and him getting dressed in his black uniform and leaving immediately with just a small kiss on her head, she felt like she had him back.

Hell, she felt like she had herself back.

She sat up in her bed and took her phone from the bedside table. She had two texts and a missed call. She looked at the caller and pressed the green button to return it.

"Oh my giddy aunt, I feel vile."

April laughed as Amelia sounded how April felt. Sore in more places than not.

"Amen to that. I don't know about you, but I didn't stop throwing up until about nine last night. Ellie was upchucking after that still as well. All the way up until Ethan picked her up from my room."

"Urgh, I know how she feels. Any word from Vick? She looked toxic green when I left her at hers and Steve's room."

"She has text me but I haven't read it yet. I fell back to sleep after Andrew left: I've just woken up."

"You're sooooo lucky. I woke to the sound of Drew exercising his vocal chords at seven thirty this morning."

"Rather you than me. So, do you know what's going on?"

"Not really. All I know is a car was on its way to the building this morning, Lucas was meeting Andrew in the tech lab and they were all meeting the rest of the Soldier's in the gym at nine. Lucas hasn't been back since."

"Yeah, Andrew hasn't. I hope everything is ok."

"I'm sure it is. If I know Lucas and Andrew they'd prevent world war three today to ensure Chris, Tony and Simon have a good send off."

"I know. I can't believe it's finally happening you know. We will finally lay them to rest."

"It's been a long time coming. What you wearing?" April smiled; it was never too far away on the agenda. Amelia always wanted to know what everyone else was wearing so she could coordinate and not look either too over, or too under dressed.

"Probably a black dress, black heels."

"Yeah yeah, me to."

April heard Drew crying in the background.

"Ape's I've got to go. Devil child is throwing a paddy because he can't get his whole hand in his mouth."

April laughed, "no worries. I'll see you at the common room at three."

"Date…" Amelia hung up.

April scrolled through her phone to read the text she had from Ellie.

If I look like I'm going to throw up today, move me away from people will you. See you at the common room at three xxx

April smiled and text back… *I'll push you behind a tree somewhere: all good xoxo*

She then looked at the text she had from Vicky.

I knew mum and dad swayed us away from alcohol for a reason. I feel like I want to curl up in a cold bath and shiver this out. My thoughts will be with you today. I'll meet you at the common room at three sis. Much love x

April text back… *I know how you feel. I think all of us are with you there today Hun. See you at three, thanks for the thoughts. Love you always xoxo*

April sighed. Today's funerals were just another reminder of the life she was living. A life where people died because of her, a life of being fearful of something going wrong, a life full of bollocks with her at the centre.

She tried to shrug it off. Repeating Andrew's words in her head that this wasn't her fault, and she should stop feeling guilty. She'd said the same words straight back at him last night and hoped it sunk into him as much as he wanted it to sink into her.

She got out of bed and went over to the wardrobe in her and Andrew's antique and refined room and started looking through her black dresses. Finding a respectable knee length, long sleeved and Bardot style dress, she got out her black winklepicker heels and lay them on the bed. She showered, put a small amount of makeup on knowing today would be filled with tears and any amount of mascara would be running down her face, and checked the time on the clock on their TV stand. One in the afternoon.

She grabbed her phone and went to ring Andrew. He hadn't been back at all, and she was starting to worry. He picked up on the second ring.

"Everything ok love?"

"Yes, same with you? You've been gone a while."

"I know. You also won't believe what happened this morning. Yesterday Jamie managed to put a tracker on a car that picked your EX up from the airport. Today that car drove to our compound, the guy driving had been beaten severely by your EX and his partner in crime and told him to send us a message. Little did they know he had his phone recording the whole time. We know everything. We know how to stop it and when. It all ends tomorrow morning babe. That I promise you now."

April was in a state of shock. She should be pleased; she should be shouting from the rooftop that this was nearly all over: she just couldn't. She sat there quiet, not knowing what to say or how to act.

"Love, you still there?"

"Yes sorry. I don't know what this means."

"It means your EX has hurt too many people in the process of his plans. It means he thinks he's on top, but it's backfired. From what I can gather, the guy that drove here today lost his brother back when the bomb nearly killed all of us. He has been pushed around, beaten, relied upon to do the dirty work and he's had enough of it all. He's an ally. I know I've promised you in the past this will end, we will win: I know that to be true now."

She smiled. Finally, all her EX-husband's scheming, all his hate and all the death was rebounding on him like a karma boomerang.

"When will you be back?"

"Open the door." He hung up.

April got up and opened the door to their room. Andrew stood there with a red rose in his hand and a huge grin on his face. It lit up his eyes, it softened his features, and she went weak at the knees.

He bowed to her as he held the rose out for her to

take. "My lady."

She laughed and took the rose. She put it to her nose and smelt the flowery scent of its petals. She smiled as Andrew straightened himself back up.

"What's brought this on?" she asked.

"I think it's about time me and you got back to normal isn't it." He winked.

She nodded. Yes, yes it was.

Andrew walked into the room and closed the door behind him. He stood by the bed and watched her as she lay the rose down on her work desk.

"You look stunning love."

"Thank you."

"I was also hoping you wouldn't be ready yet. I need a shower." He winked again. She knew his agenda immediately.

She started taking off her dress and her black underwear, she tied her hair up and walked past him to the bathroom. He watched her shapely figure sway with each step and licked his lips.

"You don't need to tell me twice." She laughed.

He followed her into the bathroom and devoured her.

CHAPTER 16

"Thank you for this. We owe you a debt." Lucas said to the guy who was now connected to a drip of both fluids and painkillers and wrapped in bandages. They really had done a number on him.

He nodded and smiled. "Thanks for taking care of me."

"You're welcome. Calvin…" Lucas called out to his main medical lead.

Calvin walked around the corner wearing his white doctor jacket and with his blonde curtains covering his blue eyes.

"Boss?"

"Please keep an eye on young William here. I'm sorry to ask for you to miss the funeral but I need to ensure he's kept alive."

"It's fine Boss: I've had enough time with Chris and his team in the morgue: I've said my goodbye's."

Lucas placed a hand on Calvin's shoulder, "thank you. Radio if you need anything. May I ask for the time between three thirty and four you call upon Jamie. I'll be delivering the service."

Calvin nodded before going back to where he came from. Lucas took one final look at the state of William in the bed and walked to his room.

Today was the epitome of weird. William coming to him and telling them everything, Andrew getting back to himself with a chip in his walk and things seeming to go to plan. The caterers had arrived and he'd let Richie, Blake and Ethan take the lead on it. Steve and Jamie had their teams out on patrol, everyone else was ready to meet in the common room at three before going outside to the service, and the graves were ready for the caskets. The only thing left to do was for him to get ready and try and keep it together when he read out his eulogy.

All was quiet as he headed to his room. He punched in the code twice before the door opened and he was pleased to see Drew awake and playing in his highchair and Amelia ready to go as well. He took a moment to really appreciate what he had. He'd been lucky with Amelia. Yes she was the first auction and yes their beginning was hard on both of them, but he loved her more than life itself. She looked up from her chair and dazzled him with her smile.

"You're back."

"It would appear so my love."

He walked over to her and stood her up to take a good look. She had on a black silk blouse and a high waisted black skirt with high black heels to match. She looked like a million bucks.

He kissed her so fervently she lost her breath.

"What was that for?" she asked when he released

her face from his grip.

"I love you. Can't a man kiss his wife without reason?"

She blushed, "well yeah but you haven't kissed me like that since our wedding day."

He gave another brief kiss on her lips and walked to the bathroom. He turned just before closing the door.

"You'll be keeping that skirt on in bed tonight." He winked. Amelia blushed brighter and hotter than the surface of Mercury.

While the hot water was running over Lucas's body, he kept replaying the recording William had in his head. Unbeknown to Matt and that other bloke, Jo, William had had his phone in his pocket on record from the moment he arrived in the flat. Their plan was for William to act like he was betraying them and give the message over: after so much maltreatment William did betray them and recorded the entire plan Matt had created. He was in for the revelation of his life tomorrow morning. Lucas wondered if he'd have anyone to plan his funeral. That, he doubted.

Thinking of funerals, he really hoped he didn't mess up today. Everyone was counting on him to ensure the right words were said about Chris and his team. He'd been planning what he was going to say from the moment he decided to deliver the service, but thinking on it now, he knew he would speak from the heart. Chris had been such a part of the team for so long he felt like family. Andrew and

Lucas, Ethan and a few of the original Soldier's had known Chris from the start. He'd come in, set the tone on the diet everyone was going to have, didn't ask for permission on what to order and when, he didn't even care about the budget. His main priority was ensuring they had enough food to sustain their ability to do their role and had set the tenor for mealtimes. The kitchen was his own army, and he ran it like a Major.

There was a knock on the door. Lucas turned off the water as Amelia walked in.

"You gonna be much longer? It's two, twenty babe."

"No, just finishing up now. Love, can you get my black suit trousers, my black shirt and black tie out the wardrobe for me please?"

She nodded and shut the bathroom door.

Lucas dried himself off and left the steam of the room to get dressed. His nerves were running riot. He was nervous about delivering the service, nervous about tomorrow and nervous about the outcome of all this.

Once dressed he picked up Drew, gave Amelia a kiss on her cheek and led the way to the common room. It was now ten to three and everyone would be gathering, waiting for him to arrive. He needed to put on his leader head: he needed to get his poker face ready.

CHAPTER 17

Lucas rounded the corner to the common room. He hadn't expected to see so many people there already. Everyone was there: Andrew and April, Ethan and Ellie, Vicky and Steve, Blake, Richie, Jamie, three of the Quad, most of the Special Skills Team and a few of the longer serving Prevention Soldier's. This was probably most of everyone that was coming: a lot of other teams had been asked to work patrols around the grounds to make sure today went as smooth as possible. Most of the medical team were looking after William. This was it, and that alone was a solemn thought. They should have all been given the opportunity to be here today: everyone loved Chris equally, no one should be missing this.

As he walked into the room Sheila came over to him and held her hands out for Drew.

"Give him to me Boss, you both need today. I've got little one under control."

Drew started eagerly trying to get out of Lucas's arms and into Sheila's. He loved Sheila.

"Are you sure?"

"Of course, Boss. I have a feeling you have your

work cut out for you today and I haven't seen this little guy properly for, let me think, two days!" she started tickling Drew's belly and his laughs brought a smile to everyone's face.

With Drew now safely in Sheila's hands, Lucas went to walk over to the table at the back that had pre-poured flutes of champagne. He picked one up, took another one and gave it to Amelia and coughed to get the rooms attention.

Everyone turned to face him. He took a quick look at the sea of sad faces and the abundance of black outfits facing him and took a breath.

"Thank you all for coming today. It's been a long time coming but I feel it's better that we're all here and can fully say goodbye to Chris and his team. The plan of the day is to have a pre drink here, Calvin has sorted out the grave sites and the caskets are ready to be laid. We'll have a short service around the grave sites themselves and then we have a buffet style wake for the afternoon going into the evening. I do not want any talk about work today and I do not want too many tears. Chris was a valued member of the team for so long, I want him remembered in a way that brings joy to us all…" he raised his glass. "To Chris, Tony and Simon" He saluted, and everyone raised their glass to join him.

Once everyone had taken a drink, Lucas addressed them again, "if you'd all like to follow me please." He took Amelia's empty hand, more for his own comfort than hers, and led the way out of the building. They went through the kitchen area to the back door that led out to the grounds. This was all feeling a little too familiar for Lucas as he gazed around him. Table after table had serving plates of food covered by tin foil, there were open boxes of beer: wine and champagne were in bottle coolers with ice and April and Andrew's wedding day felt like it was being relived. For everyone's sake: he hoped it wasn't. He hoped Déjà Vu was the worst thing that would come of this evening and after-noon's events.

Upon everyone pooling out of the doors and fol-lowing Lucas to the grave sites, Lucas took a mo-ment to check his notes from his trouser pocket. Amelia put her arm around his waist and gave him a squeeze before leaving to stand by Jamie's side. At the head of the three grave sites Lucas waited for everyone to gather round. Each casket was already in the grave with the soil leaving the coffins un-covered. Calvin had done himself, and everyone proud. Each coffin was traditionally shaped and carved out of elm wood. Each had a single red rose laying on it and a picture of who was in-side it. Lucas grit his teeth: he had to or he would have teared. His men did not need to see him break down today. They needed his strength: they needed his leadership.

He took one final look at the notes he'd been re-peatedly rehearsing in his head and put them in his pocket. He didn't need them.

Everyone was silent, waiting for him to say something. He noticed Andrew holding April's hand while she wiped her eyes, Ellie was leant into Ethan who was also wiping his eyes. Looking at everyone now, there wasn't a dry eye in the place.

"I know we're all grieving today. I had prepared a whole speech, I'd rehearsed my lines but I feel I need to speak to you all from the heart. Chris was like family. He cared about us all, he never complained, he'd seen some awful things in his time here with us and was truly a gentleman. Only to speak to him was to love him. Most of you won't know this but Chris joined us in the very early days after his wife had been murdered. I'd never spoken of it before, but it was one of his main reasons for wanting to join us. On his CV he stated, that if he could have a job in an organisation that prevented what happened to his wife happening to anyone else, then his life was worth living. Needless to say, we took him on without any questions asked and time after time he proved his worth. Chris felt like a brother to some of us, a father figure to others but more than that, he was a friend. I know we will all miss him dearly."

Lucas stopped for a second to catch his breath. He looked at Andrew who was holding it together. Andrew gave a single nod to Lucas. He'd been at Chris's interview that day all those years ago: this was reminiscing in its truest form.

"Tony joined ranks only a couple of years ago..." Lucas carried on, "as did Simon. Chris mentioned that as the Solider team expanded, his team needed to grow as well and so he started scouting out local restaurants to head hunt anyone that looked their weight in gold. He came across Tony in an Italian restaurant. Sure he looked a little undertrained and gothic should I say politely, but Chris said as soon as he tasted his homemade, authentic Italian focaccia with olive oil and roasted pine nuts, he knew Tony would have the job. Simon's story was similar, only he was working at a local bakery and it was his hot cross buns that drew Chris in. Between the three of them I've had more meals from different countries than I would have gotten if I would have travelled the world and I am extremely thankful for that. I am also truly grateful that we all got to spend so much time with them all. My only regret is they were taken from us too soon."

Lucas finished speaking and looked to Amelia. She had tears streaming down her face. She blew him a kiss and mouthed 'I love you.' He smiled. It was all he could do to stop himself from joining her in her crying: joining *everyone* in their crying.

"Does anyone else have anything they would like to say?" Lucas addressed everyone. He looked at Andrew. Andrew Shook his head no: Lucas could see his eyes shining, he was trying not to let the tears fall.

Ethan was the only one to raise his hand to speak, "to be honest Boss, I think you've said it all. All I want to say is goodbye to some of the best men I knew. You'll forever be in our thoughts."

That was the straw that broke the camel's back. All of the girls burst into tears, as did some of the men. It was the saddest event Prevention had ever been through.

CHAPTER 18

Matt had spoken to around eight different members of the Hedonist group today, describing his plan and what William was currently doing. They all laughed at him. He'd lost the respect and the loyalty of all of his men. He couldn't count on Jo either. The bloke was a side dish short of a main meal and each time he'd placed an element of responsibility in Jo's hands, he'd washed it down the drain and fucked up. Matt realised he was on his own and if all of this went tits up, he'd only have himself to blame: that's if he even survives. *He* would have to plant the bomb and detonate it, *he* would have to fight Andrew to the death and *he* would have to kill April. Only then may his reputation be salvaged; only then could he move on.

Jo came out of his bathroom and sat on the couch. Matt was stood looking out of the window, where he had been since the moment William got in Jo's car and left.

"Do you think they've killed him?"

"I don't care if they have, I only care if he managed to get there and deliver my message." Matt hissed.

"What if they don't believe him?"

"They will. I sent him there bloodied and bruised for a reason. I know William has been wanting out for a while. He probably told them the entire plan. That it was a set up and to expect me to carry out what I've told him I would do."

"Won't you then?"

He turned to face Jo head on, "would you? Actually, you *would* be stupid enough to trust William has done only as we asked of him. He hasn't just pretended to betray us Jo, he has betrayed us and I was hoping he would."

Jo looked confused. "But you said…"

"I don't care what I said. If I know *how* her fella and his leader work, they'll act as if they are following the plan. They'll appear to let April and Andrew come on their own, but they won't be alone, and I'm counting on it. I'm going to set up a series of trip wires around the building and the grounds attached to grenades: one wrong slip of the foot and they're done for. I know where in the building they'll try to hide but when the grenades go off, they'll be blocked from getting out. Only when I've managed to filter them out to nearly nothing, and when her and him are close enough to the main door, will I set off the last bomb. By the time I'm finished with them, there won't be anyone left to come and save them. I'm going to drug him to make him weaker, I'm going to slit his throat and then kill her."

"What do I do?"

"You aren't going to do anything."

"Why not?"

"Because you're lacking in the brain department Jo: no doubt a product of all the steroids you've taken over the years. You can't be trusted with anything." Jo huffed and looked away. Matt returned to looking out the window. Jo was glad he wasn't needed for this. He only prayed that William did betray them as they'd discussed and tell them everything. Jo knew enough about them that they were better trained and organised than Matt thought. His ability to underestimate them had blown up in his face time after time. Jo only hoped this time, it killed him.

CHAPTER 19

The service for Chris and his team had gone better than Lucas could have ever hoped for. It was now seven in the evening, and everyone was well on their way to getting inebriated. Only a few key people such as him, Andrew, April, Ethan, Jamie, Steve, Tom, Craig, and Colin were going tee-total tonight. They had a long night ahead of them: they were about to put an end to April's EX and the havoc he'd played on Preventions lives.

Lucas had been walking around the different groups of people, catching the tail end of stories about Chris and his team. There were laughs, some horrified looks of embarrassment and some tears to join the noise of people eating the buffet food and chinking their glasses together in a toast for the long lost.

Andrew caught Lucas looking around the room and stepped away from April, Jamie, Ethan, Steve, Ellie, Vicky and Amelia.

"Not long now." Andrew said to Lucas.

"I know. I don't want to hurry anyone up, but we've got a long night and a difficult morning ahead of us."

"I know Lucas but right now, all we can do is stay here and remember our friend. You did well during the eulogy."

"Thanks, I went a little off record but I think it fitted."

"It fitted perfectly. Come and have at least one drink. I've not seen you eat or drink anything since the service started."

"You're right. Let me grab a beer and I'll come and join you all."

Andrew nodded and stood back in the circle of people he'd moved away from. He got back in the group in between April and Amelia.

"He ok?"

"Yes Amelia, he's grabbing a beer then joining us." She smiled.

April leant closer to Andrew's ear, "are *you* ok?" she whispered. He nodded.

"Yes love. You?"

She nodded back. They were not ok, both of them knew it. If one of them was worried about the night and morning they had yet to face, then the other one was equally as worried. Now was not the time to speak of it, it was not the time to think of it.

"Fucking hells and bells you won't know this Jamie, Blondie, Ells or Vick, but back in the day after Tony had been here for only two weeks..." Ethan cut off his story as Lucas joined them and put his arm around Amelia's waist. He took a swig of the bottled beer in his hand.

"Don't tell me. Is this the one where Chris found

Tony..."

"Don't spoil it Boss. Let the pro deliver the show will ya!"

Lucas and Andrew both rolled their eyes but let him have his moment.

"So, as I was saying before I was so *rudely* interrupted, Tony had been here for literally weeks. Chris had left him in the kitchen to stir some massive pot of something, I can't really remember what it was right now, but he'd literally been out of the room for minutes, but in those minutes, Tony had managed to set himself on fire and his trousers were burning."

"Set himself on fire?" Jamie asked, relishing every word Ethan was saying.

"Yeah..." Ethan carried on, "literally on fire. He'd dropped the ladle at the back of the hob, leaned over to get it and Tony's crotch went up like the fifth of November. The smoke alarms went off, everyone run back into the kitchen and all we saw was Chris throwing jugs of water on Tony's privates, Tony hopping up and down as his hairs were being singed and the smell of it was vile. By the time the flames were put out, Tony had such a huge hole in his clothes from the fire, that you could see his dick. We called him 'fire dick' for months after that."

Everyone was guffawing, including April and the girls.

"What a way to pass probation mate..." Ethan said before he continued to laugh so hard he had tears running down his cheeks.

"That's nothing, do you remember the time Simon brought a girl back and had her over the booze cabinet out the back and Chris caught them?" Andrew said.

"Oh, bloody hell yeah I do. Simon had been so surprised to see Chris stood there with his arms folded in pure rage that Si had sullied his precious cabinet, that he pulled out of the woman so quickly she lost her balance, hit her head falling to the floor and we had to call Calvin to sort her out." Lucas finished off the story Andrew had started.

Everyone was almost bent over in tears by this point. There really had been some crazy times in the Prevention kitchen that would be Chris's legacy.

The rest of the small group carried on sharing their memories of Chris and his team while other groups around the building did the same. They needed to get this off their chests: they needed one moment of happiness on a day that was downright wretched.

CHAPTER 20

It was midnight. As Lucas had instructed, April, Andrew, Jamie, Ethan, Steve, Colin, Tom and Craig had met Lucas, Blake and Richie in the tech lab. All of them, apart from Blake and Richie had their blue camouflage on. All of them had guns, knives and bullet proof vests. No one was going down tonight. The plan was clear. Get there, suss out the area, hold up in hiding and wait for April's deranged EX to show himself.

Lucas had a map out on the table and the eleven of them were in a circle around it. Blake was laying down some key points. He pointed to a red cross on the map.

"This is the warehouse William mentioned he would be. I've managed to pull up the blueprints and it's got two levels and two exits." He walked over to his desk and brought over a piece of paper. He laid it on the map. It was a detailed picture of the building itself. "This is the way in," he pointed to the front of the building that looked like it had been abandoned for ten years. "The old factory workers would come in this way, walk up these stairs to their offices and cloak rooms..." he pointed to what he was talking about, "and then back down to the main level. It's an old printing warehouse. You've got another door here," again he pointed to it on the picture, "that is the emergency exit. My guess is April's EX..."

"Bastard..." Ethan said under his breath, Lucas frowned at him before Blake carried on.

"My guess is he'll plant a bomb here," he pointed to the main entrance corridor, "if it goes off it'll block anyone getting in or out that way. My other guess is he'll be up in one of these rooms," he pointed to a single office and a large room on the top floor, "they have a clear view of the staircase so anyone going up it needs to go up carefully. He could be waiting to pounce."

Jamie nodded, "ok, is there anywhere in the building we can hide?"

"Yeah, here and here..." Richie was the one to point to a small corridor that led the way to the wash facilities on the top floor and another room on the bottom floor that might have been used for any spare parts for the machines. "I reckon he'll probably know these places but that's the best you've got. He's picked his grounds well. He knows what he's doing."

Lucas nodded in agreement to Richie's statement. It would appear he did know what he was doing. It was open plan and if he was already holding up in the building, they would be spotted entering from all angles. He had the higher ground on this. They needed to be careful.

"I suggest Jamie, Colin, Craig and Tom find a way to get in that room downstairs. It might be worth opening the emergency exit and leaving it half closed so we have a quick escape if we need it. Me, Ethan and Steve will try and get upstairs tonight and lay in wait. That way if we're already there and he turns up after, we're in position to fight. Andrew and April, you're going to go in the front of the building as he thinks you are. We'll try and make out we're following his plan, but we'll have him surrounded."

Lucas looked at April, "are you ready for this," he raised a brow to her.

She looked at Andrew, took his hand and looked straight back to Lucas. "Yep: let's kill the bastard."

Lucas and Andrew smiled: Ethan slapped her on the back in an affectionate gesture. "Now you're talking blondie."

Lucas looked at Richie. "Did you inform the local Police of what's going on."

"Yeah Boss, they are going to clear the building closest for safety reasons and leave you to it. They said they'd be on standby if you need them."

"Thank you, let's hope we don't. So, everyone clear on their role?" Lucas slowly swept his gaze around the nine Prevention Soldiers who were going to end this once and for all. They each nodded. They were ready: ready to face this down: they were ready to come out on top. Failure wasn't on the cards tonight. They *had* to win: they *had* to kill him.

"Move out then team. We'll take two cars. Jamie, Tom, Craig and Colin you'll ride with me in the Land Rover, Ethan you'll go with Steve, April and Andrew." Again, they all nodded.

"Radio check. Line one guys."

Everyone took the radio off their belt and turned it to line one. Lucas headed the way out of the room and to the cars: Ethan was the last one to leave. He stopped for a second to look at Blake and Richie, "hopefully we'll all be back in one piece. Should anything happen to me and Steve, tell Ells and Vick we love them and we went down fighting."

Richie nodded, as did Blake. "You'll be back though, we wouldn't be that lucky to get rid of you," Blake said, and Ethan laughed. He left and followed everyone else down the main stairs, out the front revolving doors and to the cars. This was it: there was no going back now. Lucas only hoped they got there before April's EX did. If he was there already, Lucas doubted this plan would work, hence why they were going in the middle of the night to catch him off guard.

CHAPTER 21

It was one in the morning and Matt was setting his traps. He'd set up a wire that would trip a small explosion in the corridor at the front entrance to the building. He'd done the same thing with the emergency exit door and the small room off the floor downstairs. Outside were three more trip wires. He was now in the main office on the top floor, checking his surroundings and looking out the window.

He'd chosen his stadium well. He could see anything that was happening around the area, clearly for miles. He could see the entrance to the building from up here and the only other entrance had been set up so much so, to alert him if anyone tried to open it. The trip wires around the grounds would set off a chain reaction, activating all the bombs apart from the one in the front corridor. He held the detonator to that himself. He smiled. He was more than pleased with himself. He'd been able to wangle these pieces of equipment from one of his old mates: he nearly roped him in to help but thought better of it. He didn't need anyone else's help anyway. He was so sure of himself, so convinced he'd win, he didn't want anyone else able to take the credit for his master plan.

As he carried on looking out the windows, he saw a couple of Police cars pull up. Ten Officers piled out of the two cars and started running toward Jo's block of flats. Immediate panic settled in. He took his phone out and called Jo. He didn't answer. He called again and again. Finally, when Jo picked up the call, more than five minutes had passed. In that five minutes Matt could see people walking out of the building and far away from the warehouse he was in.

"Fucking hell Jo, why can't you answer the phone. What's going on over there?"

"The Police are emptying the building. Someone's called in a bomb threat."

Matt grit his teeth. This was the first part in their retaliation then. This was them, activating their own plan. They were here. He could feel it.

Matt squeezed the phone in his hand.

"Where are they taking everyone?"

"They just finished knocking on my door. I've been told to leave immediately and leave my belongings behind. I've been told to go to the closest hotel or with any close by relatives."

Again, Matt grit his teeth. His jaw hurt from the pressure. He tried to control his breathing that was now rapid and deep. He was livid. He knew they had connections with the local Police, but he didn't quite grasp the relationship they had with them and what the Police were willing to do for him and his fucking leader. He hung up the phone to Jo.

He carried on looking out of the window as family after family and person after person were evacuated from the building. Forty-five minutes later and the area was empty of people. Even the Police cars had gone.

He started pacing around the room. Where were they? He knew they were here. Why else would the Police have come? What were they playing at? What was their angle?

He went back to the window. Bingo. They *were* here. He could see Andrew and April slowly walking to the front entrance with their guns held up, ready to shoot.

He took a moment to look at April. Really, look at April. Her hair had grown longer and seemed even blonder than he remembered. He didn't want to admit it, but she looked good. Dressed in a blue camouflage uniform, she looked well trained, slimmer and confident. Something he never thought he'd see. She was nothing but a scale breaker when he was with her. It was one of the reasons he'd slept with someone else behind her back. At the time she repulsed him. He didn't feel that way looking at her now.

CHAPTER 22

After the Police had sent a text to Lucas's phone stating the area was clear of people, Lucas looked at his team.

"We're good to go," he said, and looked straight at Andrew. His jaw was tight, his eyebrows were low and his eyes held an element of rage. He was so close to her EX, closer than they'd ever been before: he knew Andrew was itching to kill him.

"Filter out and good luck. We'll meet at the end."

The already divided teams started walking to their locations. All of them had their guns out.

Steve, Lucas, Ethan, Jamie, Colin, Craig and Tom all walked round the back of the building. They had a feeling April's EX was already there and that he would be watching the front entrance like a hawk. They'd planned to get in round the back, for four of them to hold up in the downstairs room they suggested earlier and the other three to try and get in the building and wait near the bottom of the stairs. Lucas knew that as soon as April and Andrew entered the warehouse, Matt would set off the bomb that would keep them all out. At least this way, if they were inside, they could help. Lucas's earlier plan of getting up the stairs and holding out in the upstairs corridor was a good idea, but it took the Police so long to get there and evacuate the apartment block, he knew April's EX would have been alerted something was going on. Lucas knew he was already there: already waiting. They had to change their plan on the spot, but it was still a good plan all the same.

April and Andrew held back for a while, waiting for the signal to come through the radio that Lucas and the rest were in the building. While waiting, Andrew looked at April. She looked terrified. She looked as though she had no faith in this plan working and it speared his heart. He would kill her EX and make him pay for everything he had done to her, and believe it, the list was long. He'd married her under false pretences, he'd cheated on her and got someone else pregnant, he'd been involved in Andrews kidnapping in the very beginning, he'd arranged for April to be taken from town, he'd killed Brian and Pete, even Scott was *still* recovering from that fatal day as well. He then took Ellie and nearly killed her, he'd been tracking April the whole time, he'd ruined their wedding day and he'd killed Chris, Tony and Simon. The guy's list of victories was almost quite impressive, if it hadn't of been April who was the key to it all and the one who kept losing the people she loved.

He was just about to move near to her and take her hand to give her some reassurance, when Lucas radioed in.

"Andrew you there?"

"Yeah Lucas, you in?"

"No, we've hit a snag. He's tripped the back exit. If I touch this thing it's going to go up. If he doesn't know we're here already, he will after this thing goes off."

Andrew growled. He was losing all thoughts of diligence. He looked at April. She knew. With just that one look on Andrew's face, she knew they were about to do this alone. She nodded and took her gun out. She checked the mag, took it off safety and winked at him.

"Lucas, we're going in."

"Andrew don't you da......."

Before Lucas could finish what he was saying, Andrew turned his radio off. It was now or never. Andrew would rather dine with the devil himself in the morning, than not go through with this tonight. He took out his own gun, did the same safety checks as April had and took the lead.

"Stay close to me love," he said over his shoulder as she was following his every footfall. She did as he asked and watched carefully how he positioned his steps. He was like a prize-fighter, lithe on the balls of his feet, keeping his balance but at the same time he was like a coiled cobra, ready to strike at any moment. April was slightly awed if she was honest with herself. She'd never seen Andrew in action like this before. In training she had, but not in the field.

Both of them walked close to the wall of the evacuated building, where they'd all been hiding out of sight from the warehouse. Andrew kept a watchful eye on the windows in the warehouse they were headed to, and also on the ground and area below. He would bet his life that if the back door to the warehouse was tripped with a wire and a bomb, then other parts of the building and area were as well. He wouldn't accidently blow them both up because he wasn't being vigilant enough.

CHAPTER 23

Matt carried on watching April and Andrew get closer and closer to the entrance. He could picture what he'd say to her, what he'd say to them as a couple. He could see in his mind's eye Andrew lying on the ground, bleeding from the jugular and her crying on her knees. He could see him shoot her in the head and finally get his reputation back. It would be over soon. He knew it would. He just had to get through this without his feelings for her getting in the way. She had to die. It was always the plan. She was meant to die years ago: his stringing her along was a convenience but his feelings for her kept growing. He needed to push them to the side. He needed a clear head. He needed to win the war.

He kept walking up and down the windows to the office at the top of the building. He could see the group of men they brought with them. He could see them there, trying to find a way to deactivate the bomb but he knew they wouldn't succeed. The wire itself was connected to a bomb inside. The only way to stop it was to get in the building, but the only way to do that was to open the door they were standing in front of and that would only cause the bomb to go off. He laughed. He'd done himself an honour on this. He could see one of them scratching their head in thought, he could see two others pacing up and down and one man trying to get round the front and another stopping him. The other two just stood there looking like spare parts.

He walked back to the front of the windows where he could see the entrance. They were nearly inside. Just one more meter then he would press the detonator in his hand. The corridor would go up behind them, keeping the three of them in and everyone else out. Just a few more steps: three, two, one…..

He pressed the button on the small charge operator in his hand and covered his ears.

CHAPTER 24

"I don't like this Boss. We need to get round the front." Ethan kept trying to leave the group behind and run to April and Andrew's aid.

Lucas kept stopping him.

"He's made his choice on this Ethan and the best thing we can do right now is figure out how to get in this fucking building."

Ethan huffed. He didn't like this. He didn't like waiting. He needed to go to April and Andrew. He needed to see if they were ok. Ellie knew what they were planning to do tonight. She'd asked only one thing of him, 'bring my sister back to me.' He wouldn't fail Ellie: he would *not* fail blondie.

"Boss I can't..."

"Ethan give it a rest will you. There's nothing you can do now. Let Andrew deal with this."

"What if that idiot gets her killed. Weren't you the one who had me and Jamie looking after him the last few days? Weren't *you* the one who was worried about his state of mind?"

"Yes, but Andrew knows what he's doing. And like I said, the best thing was can do is get...."

BOOM.

Lucas stopped talking. His face dropped. All they heard in the quiet of the night was the sound of a building caving in on itself. A bomb at the front entrance had gone off. There was no time.

"Ethan, Steve, Jamie, with me NOW...." He shouted. He started running around to the front of the warehouse, praying that the building hadn't fallen on top of Andrew and April: praying they had at least got inside unharmed.

As he was running he turned and shouted to Tom, "get that fucking door open: even if you have to blow it."

Lucas waited until Tom put his hand up, signalling he'd heard him, and then he carried on running. He would not let Andrew or April die today. He'd never live with himself if he did.

CHAPTER 25

Andrew and April couldn't stop coughing: they could barely breath. They'd managed to get in the building just in time before the small explosion caused the corridor entrance to cave in on itself. There was dust in the air, Andrew's ears were ringing from the shock wave, but he thanked God almighty they weren't harmed.

Andrew put his arm around April's waist and supported her to walk away from the devastation. She kept coughing and trying to pull dust free air into her lungs. The further they walked away from the entrance, the easier their breathing became.

"Andrew we're trapped."

Andrew looked in the direction of April's gaze. She was right. There were huge bits of debris blocking the corridor. Chunks of wall had fallen on the floor, metal from the pipes was half hanging out of the rubble itself. It would take a bulldozer to get through it.

"Are you in the building yet scale breaker?"

April's face went eerily pale. She hadn't heard that voice or that despicable name in years. Andrew could feel a frenzy of emotions inside him, welling up, bubbling to the surface. He'd never known anger like it. What fucking bloke called their Ex-wife scale breaker? Without thinking, he put his head back and roared. The sound vibrated around the building walls and kept on coming as it echoed off the emptiness.

He heard laughing coming from upstairs. He couldn't think clearly. All he could see was red: he blacked out. This wasn't any normal black out from rage either, this was something else. He was foaming at the mouth he was so incensed. His blood was boiling in his veins, his mind could only think of one thing. Die. Die you worthless piece of shit.

Andrew looked at April. He didn't have time to feel bad for her, he didn't have the time to comfort her. She stood there, still as pale as a summer's day cloud and he noticed her jaw quivering. She was about to cry.

He looked away from her. He started a slow incline up the stairs to where he'd heard that callous laugh and didn't stop to check if she was with him. His mind was reeling. He couldn't think. He couldn't tell if this was the right thing to do but all plans were abandoned now. He was led by two things. He was led by fury. He was led by hatred.

Andrew kept his footsteps quiet, though he knew it would be pointless. *He* knew they were in the building. *He* knew Andrew was coming up this flight of stairs.

Andrew's foot was just about to set down on the

very top step when he heard… "you ready for this?" He didn't have the time to answer. He thought he was. He thought he was ready to face down anything that her EX put forward, but he didn't expect this. Andrew panicked when he felt the dart go into his shoulder. He'd been hit with a tranquiliser. His eyes started spinning in his head: his limbs started feeling heavy: his legs wouldn't hold him up much longer. He hit the floor.

April had started to follow Andrew when she heard Matt talk to him. She screamed in pure horror when she saw Andrew on the floor, paralysed and unable to move and Matt dragging him by his arms across the dusty floor.

CHAPTER 26

Lucas, Jamie, Ethan and Steve had managed to get to the front of the warehouse, just in time to hear April scream.

Ethan started hauling huge bits of concrete out of the way in a blind panic.

"We have to get in there Boss." He said as he carried on his futile attempt at getting in.

Lucas started helping Ethan pick up unbelievably heavy bits rubble: Steve and Jamie were working at moving the pipes. If they could just get a small gap open to get through: if they could just get in.

Lucas stopped to pull out his radio.

"Tom what's going on?"

"Did you hear her?" he replied, his voice sounded as alarmed as Ethan's had.

"I did, what's going on back there?"

"Colin seems to think if we put a grenade at the bottom and stand back, the door will explode. My only worry is, it'll bring down more building than we want it to."

"Just do it. We're trying to get in from the other side. We HAVE to get in."

He radioed out. He started getting in the thick of it

again, helping Ethan move boulders that were half the size of small cars. It was worthless.

Lucas pulled a grenade from the utility belt he had around his waist.

"Everyone move."

Jamie saw what Lucas had in his hand and nodded approvingly. Meet fire with fire. That was the only way they were going to gain any ground on this: blowing another hole would be the only way they were getting in.

CHAPTER 27

April finished her toe-curling scream: it still rang in her ears now. She couldn't move her feet. All she could do was stare at Andrew trying his hardest to get to his knees, but he kept falling back down. He was fighting the tranquiliser, but April knew it was hard for him. His face was sweating with his exertion at trying to fight the drug that wanted to render him useless.

Matt stood over Andrew with a look of complete euphoria on his face. April couldn't let him win anymore. She had to do something. She held her gun up ready to fire: only she couldn't. *Why* couldn't she pull the trigger? Everything inside her was telling her to shoot this gun and end it all: everything was telling her that she needed to do this: that she *had* to kill him before he killed Andrew, but her fingers just wouldn't move.

"S-step away from h-him," she said. She tried to stop her voice from wavering, she tried to sound confident: it didn't portray that way.

"Him? I'm going to kill him you little bitch, then I'm going to kill you."

"Why? What have I done?" The tears overspilled:

she'd let herself down. She'd promised herself she wouldn't cry. It didn't last long, did it.

"Why does it matter? You've escaped me time after time and I won't let it happen anymore. By the time this is over, you'll be sharing a grave together."

The gun in April's hand started shaking. She was losing her resolve. She wanted to shoot him. She wanted to end his life but she couldn't think straight. She had to know why. She just *had* to.

No longer caring if she was crying or trembling in fear, she took a step closer to Andrew. She tried to gain a grip on the gun in her hand and raise it to aim it at Matt's head.

He laughed in her face. "Look at you. You weak, disgusting whore. Do you really think that's going to scare me?"

He took a lunge towards her to knock the gun out of her hand. She froze. Thankfully, Andrew had managed to raise his arm and grab Matt's ankle. He went tumbling over his own feet and April's senses came flooding back to her. She darted two meters to the right but as she did, in her quick movements of flight or fight, the gun fell out of her grip and went skidding across the room.

Matt turned to Andrew. He took out a knife from a roll under his left trouser leg and scurried on his hands and knees to place it at Andrew's neck. Andrew tried to get his strength back to stop him but it was no good. The drug was well dispersed in his system now and there was no fighting it. As Matt pulled Andrew to his knees by the hair on his head and stood behind him, the knife at Andrew's neck started drawing blood. April didn't know what to do. She saw hers and Andrew's life flashing in front of her eyes. She saw a premonition of her standing at his grave side crying for the loss of him. She saw each happy moment they had shared and couldn't believe they would share no more in the future.

"This is it April. Any final words to your beloved here?" he spat in such a vicious tone she cowered.

She dropped to her own knees and looked straight at Andrew's face. His was grey and his eyes were half hooded. She mouthed 'I love you,' and he tried to smile back. They knew this was it. Matt was about to cut open Andrew's neck so he bleeds out, then he would take whatever weapon he chooses and would kill April. She didn't have the strength in her to stop him, or to fight him off.

As the tears running down her face got caught in the thick layer of dust on her cheeks, she looked at Matt. Her eyes pleading for him to stop this: for him to let them go, let bygones be bygones.

His hand was moving the knife to the other side of Andrew's neck, ready to pull it across the front of his Adams apple in one swoop: he smiled.

BOOM.

BOOM.

CHAPTER 28

Just as the grenade went off at the front of the building, another went off round the back. Lucas pulled his hands away from his ears and waited for the dust to settle. There was a small gap. Someone could get in. He didn't know how much luck Tom and the others had, but this was good enough for him. He rushed back to the entrance, trying to fit himself through the small gap at the top of the rubble: it was in vain. He was too big.
He roared in anger. He looked back at the men with him. Jamie: he was the smallest: he could get in.
"Jamie, get in that building NOW," he bellowed.
Jamie didn't need to be told twice. He took his utility belt off; he took off anything that would prevent him squeezing through the gap and started putting his arms through first: his body swiftly followed and then his legs and feet. He fell to the ground on the other side and coughed as the wind was knocked out of his chest.
"Gun," he shouted through the gap.
Lucas tossed his Glock 17, gen4 pistol through the hole.
"Got it..." Jamie shouted and then ran towards the

stairs of the warehouse. As he climbed the stairs, he heard a scuffle at the top. He had the gun held up, ready to shoot, only he didn't expect to see what he saw.

CHAPTER 29

Matt's knees buckled at the two explosions. They also knocked the knife out of his hand. Andrew had fallen back to the ground, but this time his strength was coming back. Matt knew then, he should have used a higher dosage in the dart he shot him with. He ran away from Andrew and tried to get to the gun that April had earlier dropped. She had the same idea. She got up and ran across the room and did a rugby skid to get to the weapon before Matt could. He landed on the floor the same time she did and he punched her in the face to stop her. April's head flung back on her shoulders, but she wasn't about to let him succeed. She rolled over on to her knees and jumped on Matt's back with her arm tightly around his neck. She had him in a chokehold. She tried squeezing the life out of him, but she just wasn't strong enough.

"Andrew..." she cried out. Hoping he would help her. He was nearly to his feet but his knees kept giving way underneath him.

"Andrew please, I can't..."

She was cut off. Matt had managed to get out from

under her, pull her arm away from his neck and roll over with her underneath him. He pressed his forearm to her windpipe and started cutting off her air supply. She tried moving her legs, squirming to get him off her but it didn't help. How was he this strong? She didn't remember him being this strong!

April's eyes started to water. She started to see stars in her eyes and felt the last bits of oxygen leave her system. She was going to die.

She looked over to Andrew who was slowly walking. April could see how painful it was for him to stand, let alone bring one foot up in front of the other. He carried on, swaying on unsteady feet to get to the knife Matt had dropped. It would take him too long. He wouldn't get there, and to her, in time. This was it. April's eyes hazed over, she struggled to take one last constricted breath under Matt's arms and lost the fight.

CHAPTER 30

Jamie stood in shock. From all the things he'd seen in his life, on one tour with the army or another, this was the worst. Andrew was trying to get to a knife, but Jamie could tell he was torn. Torn between using the last of his energy to get to April who was unconscious under Matt's pressure on her neck: torn between getting to the knife and throwing it at Matt to get him off her.

Jamie held the gun up in his hand, aimed it straight at the back of Matt's head and pulled the trigger.

BANG.

Andrew looked at the sound of where the bullet had started and swept his gaze to where it had landed. Matt had now fallen on top of April. The blood from the wound in his face was dripping all over *her* face and *her* hair, staining it red underneath him. Andrew fell to the ground elated. It was over. He was dead. He only prayed April hadn't gained the victory with her life. He couldn't get up: he couldn't keep fighting the drug in him anymore. The last thing he saw before everything went black, was Jamie hauling Matt off April.

Jamie looked over to Andrew as the light left his

eyes. He cursed under his breath. He kept trying to feel a pulse under his fingers on April's neck, but nothing was pumping back. This couldn't be it: it couldn't have happened.

All his military training came back to him in a surge of urgency. He pulled April's airway back and blew two, one-second-long breaths into her lungs before starting his chest compressions.

All he could think was that they'd lost. They'd lost her. She was dead.

Jamie carried on alternating between rescue breaths and chest compressions. He stopped only long enough to see Lucas, Ethan and Steve enter the room.

Their faces said it all. They were too late and they all knew it. Ethan punched the wall: feeling a loss so profound he wanted to die himself. He'd failed. They'd all failed.

Lucas ran over to Andrew with Steve.

"Jamie what happened to him?"

"Drugged…" he said as he carried on working on April's body. Trying, in some way to give some of *his* lifeforce to her. He carried on beating down on her chest by doing his compressions, he carried on exhausting himself by giving his breath to her.

What felt like minutes went by, then as if God had granted Jamie's silent wishes, April started reaching for breath and her eyes started opening. He fell from his knees on to the back of his legs and cried. He cried in victory, in sheer happiness, in total joy. It had worked: his persistence had brought her back.

Ethan noticed the life coming back to April and he ran over to her. He fell to his knees and cradled her head in his hands. The tears falling down his face unstoppable.

"Blondie? Blondie are you ok?"

She nodded. She couldn't speak and Ethan could see why. Already she had a cracking bruise on her throat where her windpipe had nearly been crushed.

April started to say something, but no sound came out. Her voice was worse than a whisper: it wasn't there at all. Ethan looked at her mouth, trying to lip read what she was saying.

"Andrew?" he asked her.

She nodded. He looked over to Lucas who nodded and smiled at Ethan. He was alive.

"He's ok blondie. You're both ok."

A solemn tear fell out of April's left eye. It was over. They had won. In what state they would be in in a weeks' time was yet to be foreseen, but they were alive and Matt wasn't. April closed her eyes and silently wept. Victory. Now she could rest. Now she could relax.

CHAPTER 31

Even though four weeks had passed, April still felt sore. The discomfort in her neck wasn't as bad as it had been the day after she woke up in the medical ward in a bed next to Andrew, but apparently, under the direction of Calvin, the pain could take a few more days to dissipate fully.

Andrew had recovered, needing nothing more than a plaster on his neck and a drip of fluids to flush the drug out of his system.

The Police had been alerted to go back and get Matt's body: they were to cover up the situation in the news as a gas leak causing the explosions, and Prevention had been on rest since the day they came back.

April walked out of the bathroom in hers and Andrew's room in a long, strapless red dress and some killer red heels. She'd curled her hair and it fell in tight ringlets around her face and her shoulders and she'd taken the bandage off her neck. When she was doing her makeup in the bathroom, she thought about trying to cover up the faint purple of the bruise on her neck but didn't: she'd initially wanted to show it off: she'd initially wanted to let everyone know they'd come out the other side, even if the damage to her physical frame was still there. Now Andrew was looking at her, she was almost regretting not covering it up.

Andrew had been sat in their brown chesterfield chair, waiting for her to finish. He sat waiting in a white shirt, black trousers and black dress shoes and was tapping his foot on the floor. When she entered their main room, his heart took a giant thump in his chest. She was beautiful. No words would do her justice.

"Love," he said as he stood and walked over to her. "You look incredible."

She blushed, "you don't think it's too much?"

He shook his head no. He raised his hand to place two gentle fingers under her chin and lift it so he could see the marks on her neck. He frowned as he released her face and looked into her eyes.

"Love I'm so sorry."

She wrapped her arms around his waist and lay her cheek on his chest. He responded by wrapping his own arms around her and giving her a squeeze. "Don't be. I thought I'd lost you. I thought at one point you were going to die. Andrew I'm so glad it's over."

"Me too love. I just wish you didn't get harmed in the process."

He felt her shoulders shrug under his embrace. It was nonchalant.

"It could have been worse." She admitted. And Andrew knew she was right: it could have been a lot worse. They both could have died under Matt's duress, the bomb could have taken out Lucas and the rest of them and if *that* had of happened, her sisters would have lost their lovers, Amelia would have lost her husband and Drew would have lost his dad. It was almost unthinkable how differently this could have played out.

Andrew let her go and took her hands, "shall we head off?"

She nodded. She waited for him to finish lifting her hands to his lips and kissing the tips of her fingers before he let her go. She grabbed a thin red scarf and wrapped it around her neck. He took it off her. "You don't need that love: not tonight."

She smiled and nodded. She didn't know what kind of night he had planned for them both. All she knew was that she was ordered to buy a new dress, new underwear and new shoes from the internet, in preparation for tonight's activities. He'd told her to spare no expense and dress as if she was walking the red carpet. She had.

Andrew opened their door and led the way downstairs with her hand, firmly in his. April's eyes started taking in the scene in front of her. Red petals were everywhere. They seemed to start from the door to their suite, lead all the way down the hallway and carry on down the main flight of stairs. April looked at Andrew.

"Is this your doing?"

He smiled but didn't say a word.

As they were approaching the last few stairs on

the bottom floor, April heard noise in the air. She didn't know who it was or where it was coming from but there were laughs, the sound of bottles hitting each other in a toast of celebration and the warm smell of BBQ wafting in through the open windows.

Andrew led her around the corner to the kitchen. She stood in astonishment.

Everyone there was dressed in clothes so extravagant, she beamed. Her eyes took to the spectacle, and she beamed even more. They hadn't realised her and Andrew were stood at the door to the kitchen and she was thankful. She could spend all the time in the world, taking in this sight and would never tire of it.

Ethan stood in navy blue trousers and a salmon pink shirt. Ellie stood next to him wearing a short, navy mini dress that fell off her shoulders in a batwing style: she had navy open toe heels on her feet. Vicky stood with her arm wrapped around Steve's waist. He wore the common black trouser and white shirt combo and Vicky looked stunning in a knee length black dress that had a lace overlay to it.

Lucas was dressed more formal in a black suit. He had the jacket undone and his white shirt was crisp and freshly ironed, and Amelia stood next to him in a pastel pink gown that had thin straps and an open back.

Jamie stood next to a wheelchair and when April noticed who was in it, she grinned even more.

Scott sat in his wheelchair: still recovering from that frightful day a year or so ago but she was *so* glad to see him mingle with the group again. They both wore black trousers and white shirts. The Quad was there, wearing the same get up as Scott and Jamie and were teasing Scott in his wheelchair, and then she noticed someone else with them she remembered as being part of the Hedonist group. Andrew had mentioned William was now a part of Prevention: that if it hadn't of been for him, they wouldn't have known what Matt was planning. He was a part of their survival, soon to be a part of their future. The Special Skills team were there, all in their black trousers and white shirts and every single person had a glass of champagne in their hands. Most of the Quad and the Skills Team had a beer in their other hand as well. Andrew coughed loudly to get everyone's attention. Everyone stopped to look at the doorway and the smiles and cheers that erupted from the group were so loud April's ears felt the noise like a foghorn.

"Andrew what's all this?"

"This love, is a party to end all parties." He winked at her and pulled her hand gently to follow him into the room. As they walked through to reach Lucas and the gang, various people came up to them both. Some put a hand on her shoulder and smiled, Jamie gave her a kiss on the cheek in welcoming, others titled their beer or champagne towards her with a smile of relief that she was still alive. Then it was Ethan's turn.

He left Ellie's side to walk over to April and took her in a huge hug that lifted her feet off the ground. He kissed her cheek and put her down.

"Look at you all alive and kicking. Plus, don't let this go to your head but you scrub up well." He winked, she laughed.

"I'd say the same to you as well but you're still an idiot."

Ellie came over and took Ethan's hand again and looked at April. Her face said it all. She was relieved April was still alive, she was proud of Ethan for bringing her back.

"That he is sis, but he's my idiot and I love the guy." Ethan mockingly put a hand on his heart, "Such sweet words." Ellie and April laughed.

Amidst her reunion with Ellie and Ethan, she noticed Andrew head to Lucas and then both of them were walking over to the table where there were flutes upon flutes of champagne. She looked back at the group in front of her. Amelia was next in line to speak.

"You look stunning girl," she whistled.

"Thanks hun: you too. What's going on?"

Amelia acted out zipping her lips together with a key and then threw the key over her shoulder, she shrugged and moved out the way. April raised a questioning brow.

Vicky and Steve approached April this time. Steve gave her a kiss on the cheek and Vicky came in for a hug.

"You look amazing sis."

"You to, but Vick, what's going on here?"

"Can't say I'm afraid." She also shrugged her shoulders, the same as Amelia had and moved out of the way.

They all stood in a circle around April, trying not to spoil the moment. They knew something she didn't. They were all in on it, that much she could tell.

Andrew and Lucas joined them. Before Andrew could hand her the glass of bubbles he'd picked up from the table at the back, Lucas moved to kiss her cheek.

"Welcome love. You look beautiful."

"Thanks Lucas. Now will someone tell me what the *hell* is going on here?"

As Lucas moved back to stand next to Amelia, everyone looked at Andrew. He smiled and nodded to them all. He gave April the glass of champagne and left to stand at the head of the kitchen. He tapped his glass with a spoon that he'd picked up from the drinks table and waited until everyone had stopped what they were doing, and he had all of their attention.

"Everyone, I want to take a moment to thank you all. We've been through so much together and we've come out on top. We've lost some of our family, some others were harmed..." his gaze hit Scott as he said that, and Scott raised his glass higher to signal it was all worth it, "and still we all stand. I also want to thank you all for helping with today."

This time his gaze fell on April.

As she looked at him, everything else went out of focus. His gaze penetrated a part of her that she'd forgotten was there. It brought her back to life, it wiped away any fear and held a promise of a future that would be lucky and fulfilled.

"April. My love, my heart, my wife. Without you, I would have died that day in the warehouse. You managed to fight for me and our love when I was unable to do it for us and for that, I am extremely grateful. To get to this point, we've had so much taken away from us. I have arranged today to give some of that back. Our wedding day was ruined, we never got to have our reception with our friends and family and I wanted you to have that. Everyone, if you would please follow me outside."

April was near to bursting in tears. Tears of joy and tears of pure contentment.

Andrew walked over to her and took her hand. He led her out through the kitchen and past everyone, out to the back of the building and she was even more awed than she had been when she arrived to the kitchen itself.

Outside was a huge marquee. It was decorated with yellow flowers, bright fairy lights and had tables and chairs pulled up around the side of it. The main part of the marquee was a huge wooden dancefloor and there was a stage at the back. A band was getting ready to play their first song and were testing their sound effects before they started their show. April's jaw dropped in disbelief when she noticed the other people that were there. Her mum and dad, Andrew's parents, his brother Marco, her aunty Jane, Cady, Rebecca and everyone who was at the wedding the day it was destroyed, was waiting to finish it off with her and Andrew now.

Everyone outside started cheering and April's mum and Andrew's mum blew a kiss in her direction.

"Andrew I can't believe you've done this. I love you so much."

"And I, you. More than you will ever know." He bent down to touch her lips with his and every single person there cheered even more.

He let her go. "Go and see them love, I know you've been waiting for it." She smiled and run off to see their parents. Lucas walked to Andrew's side once he was on his own.

"Feels like the ending of a very bad dream doesn't it."

"Yeah, it does. We've been through so much to get to here: the look on her face when she saw her parents was worth the heartache though."

"She's a good one: I can't express how glad I am you're both here still."

For the first time in years, especially in front of the Soldier's and family, Andrew grabbed Lucas and pulled him in. It was slightly awkward in the way they were both too macho to cuddle each other, so it was more a display of patting backs than anything else, but both of them felt the 'bromance' flow through them. They'd been through so much together as a team, to come out together at the other end felt like justice for everything they had done.

Andrew let Lucas go and they both smiled. Ethan came walking over, practically crying from laughing so hard.

"That was the most awkward thing I have ever seen in my *entire* life. I feel sorry for your women if that's how you hug: they'd get more affection from a fucking teddy bear." Ethan walked away but his laughing could be heard above the sound of music that was now coming from the live band.

Andrew stood next to Lucas and they both joined in Ethan's laugh. Though he was patronising, Andrew and Lucas knew their hug felt awkward. They were men, what more could they say.

Everyone had started walking their way to the dance floor, the party in full swing now. Lucas was about to head over to Amelia when he turned on his heel and took one final look at Andrew. "I forgot to ask, did April find out why Matt did this?"

"No, she didn't, and now we'll never know."

Lucas raised his eyebrows but didn't say anything. That wound did not need reopening.

Andrew stood for just a little while longer, watching April in her element. She was laughing with their parents on the dancefloor, swaying her hips to the music and the smile on her face was so wide he'd bet her cheeks would be hurting already. He hoped this would be how she was from now on.

Happy and safe. Smiling and laughing. Free from fear. Free from her past. He would die so it could be so: if he had to, he would always put her life before his.

He spotted her scanning the crowd. Her eyes finally met his. Love. That was what her smile portrayed; it was what he knew she was feeling. He knew this because he felt it too. A love so deep they would never be separated: a love so true that it defined them both.

EPILOGUE

2002.......

"I say we start without him." Mike said, getting annoyed at having to keep waiting for Greg. He wiped the sweat off his forehead, trying to dry out the brown hair on his head. This heat was ridiculous. He sipped his beer.

"I'm good for that," Marcus replied. He too swigged his beer, wishing this summer was cooler than others before it. But it wasn't. The heat was unbearable. His brown hair was a little longer than Mikes and was sticking to the perspiration on his head.

Matt looked around the street where the three of them were sat, waiting outside the pub for Greg to arrive. The town was small. Cobble stone pathways traversed the main Highstreet, all the shops were locally owned, and it produced more of the chav population than the slums of London town.

"He's always late: it's a fucking joke." Matt said.

"Well, he's your cousin." Mike spat.

Matt rolled his eyes.

"Do you know why he called us here today Matt?" Marcus asked.

"I do, but I'll let him tell you that when he gets here."

This time Marcus rolled his eyes. Matt was as cryptic as ever.

As they carried on waiting for Greg, Matt kept looking around the Highstreet. They had a good view of the entire town outside this pub. They sat on a four-man bench without a summer umbrella and the heat was beating down on them. They all wore short sleeve baggy shirts and shorts, but that didn't stop the rays of the sun burning any inch of skin it touched.

"Just call him will you." Mike said.

Matt nodded and took his phone out of his black, shorts pocket.

Greg answered on the second ring. "You there?" he said.

"Yes, we've been here for the last twenty minutes."

"Alright, keep your hair on. Grab me a pint of Stella and I'll be there in two." He hung up.

"So?" Marcus asked.

"He'll be here in two. Drink up, I'll get the round in."

All of them downed their drinks and Mike and Marcus handed their glass to Matt: he walked into the pub to get more.

"You reckon he's up for this?" Marcus asked Mike.

"No I don't. The only reason I let him in was because Greg's his cousin and he knows how to work the system we need, otherwise I'd tell him to grow a pair and piss off."

Marcus laughed: he knew Mike didn't like Matt: that just reiterated how low his worth to the group was. Association by family and knowledge nothing more.

"Finally..." Marcus said when Greg walked around the corner to the table.

"I don't know about you, but I can't stand this fucking heat." He said to them both. Evidently as well. His white T-shirt had wet patches from sweat on the underarms and chest.

"Well, you will wear jeans when it's one hundred degrees out here."

Greg huffed and sat down. His beard was wet with sweat, the same as his hair line.

"He getting the beers in?" Greg nodded to the pub front door.

"Yeah. So, why are we here?" Marcus was more than curious to know why Greg had asked the four of them to meet here today.

"Wait until he gets back... speak of the fiend." Greg cut off.

Matt walked out of the pub with a tray holding four pints of lager. He set them down and handed each to its owner. He sat.

"Talk about me and I shall arrive." Matt laughed: Mike and Marcus rolled their eyes.

"So, spill...." Mike said, as eager to know why they were here as Marcus was.

Greg took a long gulp of his beer. "That's what I'm talking about," he said, before taking another swig and setting it down on the wooden table in front of him.

"So, do you remember those blokes I was in the army with?"

Mike nodded, Marcus looked confused, and Matt rolled his eyes.

"Don't give me them looks; this is serious."

"Well, carry on then." Mike was getting increasingly irritated.

"They have been approached by the local Government who've 'caught wind' of a potential terrorist group calling themselves the Hedonists" Greg whispered. Mike and Marcus sucked in a shocked breath. They were in the middle of creating the Hedonist group, only the Government had it all wrong: it wasn't a terrorist group as such, in the fact they were hunting and trying to auction off women.

"What do they know?" Mike asked.

"Well, from what Lucas told me, the Government have seen a separate networking site where this 'Hedonist' group have been stalking women and sharing pictures. They don't know what for, but they think it has something to do with terrorism."

"So, what else?" Marcus added.

"They've asked Lucas and Andrew to make up a team: they are giving them resources and want them to work with the local Police to keep an eye on this networking system. The idiots have asked me to be involved in it."

Mike and Marcus laughed. This couldn't be going more in their favour if it tried.

"So I assume you've said yes?"

"Of course I have Mike, I'm going to be a key player and will feedback what they're up to."

Mike took a swig of his beer in contemplation of what this meant. He put his beer back down and looked from Greg to Mike. "We need to use this to our advantage."

"I know. I can see what kind of equipment they get; can see how much they can monitor what we're doing and go from there."

Marcus nodded in agreement, as did Mike.

"So, what am I here for?" Matt piped up. The last conversation had gone over his head a little.

"I need you to find someone to follow. I need you to get her to trust you, marry her if you have to: I need you to put her across the APP and then when the time is right, we'll auction her off," Mike said.

"Why do I have to marry her, and how do I do that?"

"Just start by finding someone Matt. I don't care who it is, just find someone. You will marry her if I say you will. It'll help her feel safe and then we'll rip that safety from under her feet."

Matt huffed at Mike's tone. It was beyond patronising. Like giving a toddler something to do to keep them out of trouble.

"Ok, so how many women do we have and how many men?" Greg asked.

"I've started taking pictures of a girl local to me. Her name's Amelia. She works in the supermarket as a manager. She can be the first. We've also got about four men interested but I think we'll play the first one close to home, just to test it out." Mike answered Greg. Then Mike looked at Matt. "You got any ideas on who you want?"

He huffed again, "does it matter. It can be anyone can't it. What about her..." he pointed to a plump woman with a round face, big blue eyes, big lips and long blonde hair. She looked official in that she was wearing a white shirt with a knee length pencil skirt and black kitten heels. She had a lanyard around her neck and a black file in her hands. She was on the phone to someone as she walked past the group, sitting on their bench outside the pub.

"I suppose she'll do. So, the plan is, follow her, take photos of her, gain her trust, marry her and then we'll off her." Marcus said, with a smile so vicious Greg laughed.

"I still don't see why I have to marry her. Who would want to marry that? Look at the size of her: she'd break the scales." Matt rolled his eyes.

"Do you want the Police to have any idea you're in on this? Do you want them to start watching you? Let us not forget it's your system we're going to use. It's *your* balls if they suspect you being involved in this. At least this way if you're married to one of them who is being shared, they won't think to look twice your way."

Matt huffed again but saw Mike's point. The last thing he wanted was to have his life ruined because Greg pulled him in to this shit by asking for his knowledge on creating internet sharing systems that were private and hard to gain access to.

"It's settled then. I'll start the auction for Amelia tomorrow and Matt, you'll befriend fatty," Marcus said. He then raised his beer to the middle of the table.

"To the start of something horrifying." He laughed. Greg, Mike and Matt hit Marcus's beer glass with their own.

AFTERWORD

The end.

It's finally the end guys. The end of the book, the end of the series, the end of an era.

It took me a while to write this one: I'm not going to lie. I don't know why I found it so hard either. I knew what was going to happen, I knew in the end I couldn't let April and Andrew lose their fight but I felt so bad for April that she never got to know why. After all, that's all she wanted to know wasn't it! It was all she kept asking for in every book. Why? Why is this person doing this to me: why do they want me dead?

At least now *you* know. *You* know that she was purely in the wrong place at the wrong time. You also know that the reason for wanting her dead then, was not the same as why Matt wanted her dead in the end. A 'wrong place at the wrong time' scenario turned into hate, which turned into betrayal, which turned into revenge.

I guess after all this, maybe April was better off not knowing she was just a test pawn in the Hedonists rising. I guess, her wining will just have to be enough for her. Either way, what's done is done. I just couldn't let you guys leave this series without knowing why yourselves. I hope you agree.

As always, I'll ask you to leave a review. It's up to you whether you do or not, but it's always, extremely, appreciated. (Do you like how I just, *slipped* that in there? ha ha, wink wink, ha ha)

No, all serious now, it's been a pleasure having you read my work and hearing the amazing feedback from you all. All the best moving forward and keep yourselves safe!

ABOUT THE AUTHOR

L.a. White

I've spent a lot of time in each book, writing a little blurb about myself, telling you who I am, what I do and about my life and my job.

This time I won't.

This time I just want to express my thanks to everyone who has read this series. I've loved it, my team has loved it, my beta readers have loved it and I really hope you did as well.

Here is a picuture of April and Andrew.... ENJOY!

BOOKS IN THIS SERIES

April's Series

April's Auction - Book 1

April's Abduction - Book 2

April's Assignment - Book 3

April's Anguish - Book 4

April's Absolution - Book 5

L.a. White's Website

On this site you can see other works, character pictures and trailers!
See April's Series come to life!